Cadence of My Heart

by

Keira Michelle Telford

www.venaticpress.com

www.venaticpress.com

"I looked and looked at her, and knew as clearly as I know I am to die, that I loved her more than anything I had ever seen or imagined on earth."

-- Vladimir Nabokov, *Lolita*

IN THE DARKENED HALLWAYS OF THE SERVANTS' quarters in Neverleigh Manor, Cambridgeshire, a butler—an older gentleman in a black pinstripe suit, complete with waistcoat and polished shoes—selects an appropriate wine from the cellar to accompany the cook's menu for this evening's dinner. Elsewhere in the servants' halls, a handful of footmen check their liveries, making sure they're clean, pressed, and ready for service.

A kitchen maid in a plain blue blouse, charcoal skirt, and white apron preps vegetables at the kitchen table, while the cook pays for a fruit and vegetable delivery at the servants' entrance. In an adjoining room, a mature housekeeper with pinned up gray hair and a long royal blue dress, pores over letters of recommendation from applicants vying for a housemaid position.

A vacancy recently popped up after one of the house's senior housemaids found herself pregnant following a careless romp with one of the stable hands, and was therefore forced to leave service.

Welcome to twenty-first century Britain.

Stepping through the front doors of this elegant stately home is like falling through a time portal that throws you back two centuries. It's a romantic devolution due entirely to its relatively new owner—an eccentric American billionaire, Harlan Ashlock—who decided to recreate the Victorian era in all its glory, purely for his own amusement. Since he's also slowly acquiring country houses and estates in other counties—buying up enormous parcels of land, and even one entire village—it seems reasonable to assume that quirks like this may soon start to appear elsewhere.

Though there's no real purpose to many of the unusual things he does, his eccentricity is having certain benefits for the locals. For every place he buys, he hires a full complement of staff to manage the property and grounds, including: butlers, valets, footmen, housemaids, cooks, kitchen maids, stable hands, groundsmen, and so forth.

And it's catching on.

Privately owned stately homes up and down the country—in an effort not to be outdone by the Ashlocks—have started hiring their own domestic staff, and people are clamoring for the jobs. Affluent landowners like these can offer long-term job security, and a comfortable, live-in working environment. It's a life of hard graft, but one that's well worth the benefits it provides.

No rent.

No bill collectors.

No troubles.

Neverleigh Manor in particular—a sprawling Jacobethan-style country house that was once on the verge of collapse—now employs over fifty domestic staff, thanks entirely to Mister Ashlock and his young British wife. They used their deep pockets to fully restore the building, gave the estate a new lease on life, and secured its future for another generation with the birth of their daughter, Cadence—sole heir to the Ashlock family fortune.

Shit, Cadence!

Marlee Meeks, Neverleigh Manor's resident nanny, blows hair upwards out of her face, struggling to see the wall clock clearly. Damn. Time's up.

"I have to go." She wriggles backwards off the bed, finding her high-heeled shoes on the floor of the housemaid's sparse, undecorated bedroom. "Cadence's piano lesson just ended." She slips on the shoes, raising her from five-eight up to a clear six feet.

The unsatisfied housemaid, Rachel, a twenty-something blonde in a plain black dress and white apron, stares at Marlee in disbelief, her legs still spread on the bed.

"So that's my lot, then? You're not even gonna finish?"

"I don't have any more time," Marlee grumbles, checking her appearance in a wall mirror. "You were taking too long."

"Pardon me for enjoying myself." Rachel reaches for her knickers. "You live your whole life by that girl. Do you realize that?"

"Yes, I do." Marlee's long, honey blonde hair is too ruffled to pin back up properly, so she lets it loose. "It's my job, Rachel. I take care of her."

"She ain't a bloody toddler, Marlee. She's nearly sixteen. She won't self-destruct if she has to spend two minutes alone."

Marlee doesn't bother to argue. She's going to tend to Cadence, and that's all there is to it. Not only is it a job requirement for her to be at Cadence's beck and call, but it's a pleasure. She's likes being with Cadence, much to the confusion of the other staff who see a much greater separation between servant and master. In that way, Marlee's position is somewhat unique.

As Cadence's nanny, she's set apart from the other domestics in the household. Unlike them, she gets to sleep upstairs with the family, in the room next to Cadence's. She gets to join them for breakfast, lunch, and dinner, and often receives invites to attend family functions as Cadence's chaperone. She could also have her own assistant—a nursemaid—if she so wished, although she's never seen the need for it. She rather likes having Cadence all to herself.

Cadence is the oldest child she's ever cared for, having begun her employment with the Ashlocks little more than two years ago, when the adolescent heiress was already thirteen and a half.

At that time, the child's elderly nanny had suddenly—and rather inconveniently—dropped dead, leaving a rather large void in Cadence's care-giving, but not in anyone's heart.

The woman was, by all accounts, a crotchety old witch who'd spent far too many years on this Earth making life a misery for countless children, so nobody was much saddened by her passing—least of all Cadence. For her, it was a blessing. For her parents, it was a nuisance. For Marlee, it was little more than a fortuitous opportunity to get away from screaming babies and dirty nappies for a few years, and into a job where she could enjoy a few perks of working for one of the country's richest families.

Since her position at Neverleigh is higher ranking than that of a simple housemaid, Mister Ashlock doesn't insist that she wear the Victorian-inspired uniforms he makes the other staff wear. Instead, she's instructed to wear outfits which emphasize her womanly assets, and he'll quite boldly state to anyone who asks: "If I have to look at her, I want to *look* at her."

That means he wants to see her cleavage, it being ample and quite delightful, and his wife somewhat lacking in that department. To anyone who questions it, the answer is given that a nanny ought to exude femininity from head to toe—and Marlee surely does—although that hardly explains why her more mature, wrinkly predecessor wasn't bound to the same rules.

In compliance with the dress code, she's required to wear a selection of high heels, stockings, calf length skirts, push-up bras, and fitted blouses—the latter all having open necklines—and today's ensemble is no exception.

She fastens the buttons of her black silk blouse, adjusts her breasts within, and reaches for a stick of lipstick held by a garter at the top of one of her stockings. She applies a fresh coat to her lips, makes sure her makeup isn't smudged around her hazel eyes, then rummages for something in a beside drawer.

"Whatchu looking for?" Rachel scowls, still annoyed that she has to carry on her day without reaching sexual climax.

"Mints." Marlee keeps looking.

"Why? Worried your precious little brat will smell housemaid on you?"

"No, you just leave a bad taste in my mouth."

She follows that with a wink, but Rachel still wallops her with a pillow.

"Bugger off!"

A TORN UP MUSIC SHEET, SCATTERED LIKE CONFETTI IN the upstairs hallway, is evidence of two things: that Cadence made it to her bedroom from the music room before Marlee could make it back from the servants' quarters, and that she's in a bad mood. Crunching a mint between her teeth, Marlee stops to pick up the pieces, then knocks on the bedroom door and enters.

Cadence is lying on her bed, half curled, hugging a pillow, her back to the door. At five feet seven, the lanky teen—just shy of sixteen years old—is nearly as tall as her nanny.

Indeed, over the last two and a half years, Marlee's had the very great pleasure of watching a beautiful young woman emerge from Cadence's childish body. Her first period arrived at thirteen, not long after Marlee's arrival at Neverleigh, as if the mere presence of her delightful new nanny kick-started her body's need to reach maturity. Her budding breasts grew steadily larger—as evidenced by the constant need to replenish her underwear drawer—and the curves of her hips and ass became more prominent.

She's maturing, albeit slower in some ways than others. For one thing, she still suffers from the night terrors that have plagued her since she was five years old. Upon first moving into the house, Marlee had been instructed never to lock the cheater door between their bedrooms, lest her young charge should wake with a fright in the night.

That'd seemed silly at first. After all, don't children grow out of such things? She complied nevertheless—despite her skepticism—and was shocked one night, several months later, to roll over in bed and find a warm bundle of flesh curled up next to her.

Overcoming her surprise, she'd roused the pajama-clad teen, only to be assured that the old nanny never objected to bed-sharing. This confident proclamation was swiftly followed by a trembling lower lip and the threat of tears, the poor girl feeling rejected at the thought of being cast out into her own room.

Of course, Marlee—her heartstrings sufficiently tugged—allowed her to stay, and this became the first night of many that they slept side by side. In fact, as the months went by, it seemed that the frequency of Cadence's night terrors was increasing. When it reached the point that Cadence was spending more than four nights a week in her nanny's bed, Marlee felt obliged to make note of it to the troubled girl's parents.

Magically, however, when it was suggested that the child should see a therapist about the matter, the night terrors suddenly ceased, leaving Marlee utterly perplexed and somewhat apologetic for having made such a fuss over nothing.

Adding to Marlee's confusion, the night terrors have lately begun to reappear. Cadence still seeks comfort in her bed, albeit sporadically, but now she dare not complain. Perhaps it's related to raging hormones? Stress from school? Boys? Whatever the case, Marlee feels sure that it'll pass in its own time.

Setting the ripped music sheet on top of the dresser, she crosses the room, carefully stepping over a hastily shed pair of Converse shoes and a hoodie. Like a few other rooms in the house, Cadence's is a strange assortment of modern trappings combined with vintage décor. The bed, dresser, and sofa are antique, and the wallpaper and rug are mock vintage, but everything else is modern and doesn't pretend to be anything different. Among other things, there's a laptop, some music devices, a television, various new books, a hairdryer, and an array of contemporary clothing.

"Are you all right, Cady?" Marlee stumbles on a discarded teddy bear.

"Craaaaaamps," Cadence groans, clutching the pillow tighter. "Will you rub my tummy?" she asks, without rolling over. "Everything always feels better when you touch me."

Kicking off her slip-on shoes, Marlee moves Cadence's scruffy ponytail of long chestnut hair aside and crawls onto the bed behind her, molding their bodies together. She slides her hand over Cadence's jeans at the hip, finds them undone, and worms her fingers inside.

"How's this, darling?" She presses her hot palm against Cadence's soft abdomen, rubbing gently back and forth.

"Good," Cadence murmurs.

"It's the warmth, you know. It relaxes your muscles." Marlee kisses the side of her head, breathing in the scent of her recently washed hair. "Do you want me to fetch you a hot water bottle?"

"No." Cadence puts her hand over Marlee's, holding her in place. "This is nice. Stay."

At her wish, Marlee snuggles behind her, spooning, caressing her stomach. She's been up since before dawn, and it feels nice to lie down and relax for a moment.

Just a moment.

Or longer.

A good hour ticks by, and Marlee falls asleep, her arm draped limply over Cadence's waist. Suddenly aware of this—aware that Marlee is completely out for the count—Cadence wriggles round and repositions facing her, rolling the peaceful snoozer gently onto her back.

She wonders how old Marlee is. She's never thought to ask. Her honey blonde hair is thick and naturally wavy, usually restrained in a braid or a bun, but loose today. She'll wear it like that sometimes, when chores are light and Cadence's parents aren't around. It's a small act of rebellion against the rules and constraints here at Neverleigh.

As Cadence inspects it, she can find no hint of gray, but that might not mean a whole lot. Perhaps she dyes it. She knows her mother dyes her hair. One time, her lady's maid messed it up and accidentally turned every strand green. Cadence giggles at the memory. Her mother refused to leave the house for a week until it was properly fixed.

Turning her attention to Marlee's face, Cadence explores the faint creases at the outer edges of her eyes. So faint, barely visible. They show more when she smiles, though. So do the little laugh lines at the corners of her mouth. In contrast, Cadence ponders, the lines on her mother's face are centered around the forehead and above the bridge of her nose. They're the deep furrows of a perpetual frowner.

Marlee has a cute button nose, Cadence thinks, lightly pushing on the tip with her forefinger. She's never been sure exactly what a 'button nose' is, since the only way noses resemble buttons is that they have two holes, but if any nose could ever be described as such, it would be Marlee's. Her lips are cute, too. They're full and red, and they smell like cherries.

Cadence drags her fingertip across Marlee's lower lip, finding it soft, and viscid with a fresh coat of lipstick. Some of the lipstick comes off on her finger, and she smears it onto her own bottom lip, rubbing her lips together to spread the crimson paste around, flicking her tongue out to taste it.

Moving Marlee's hair back, exposing her neckline and chest, Cadence trails two fingers downward from her ear, feeling the steady pulse of her carotid artery below her jaw. After a brief pause, those fingers continue down, tickling lightly over Marlee's collar bone and toward her chest, her skin smooth and flawless.

Younger than Mister and Missus Ashlock, but older than some of the other staff, Cadence concludes, arriving at Marlee's bosom. Looking at her hand, then at Marlee's breasts, she assesses them to be more than a handful. But just to be sure ...

She places her hand so softly over one breast, barely making contact.

"What're you doing?" Marlee raises an eyebrow and peers at her through long, mascara-coated eyelashes.

Busted! Not to worry. This is one moment where a bit of residual childlike naïveté comes in useful, and Cadence steers herself smoothly away from any potential awkwardness.

"Why don't mine look like yours?" She presses a hand on one of her own breasts, giving it a squeeze and comparing it to Marlee's, wishing she was more than a B-cup.

"All breasts are different." Marlee yawns and stretches. "Don't give it another thought."

"Yours are epic." Cadence keeps her chocolate-colored eyes pinned to them. "They're big."

She makes another attempt to cup one of them, but, after a brief—oh, so brief—hesitation, Marlee pulls her hand away.

"You shouldn't touch me like that, darling." Her voice is warm, affectionate, and only mildly chastising.

"Why not?" Cadence pouts.

"It's ..." Marlee searches for the right word to use. "Intimate."

"So?"

"It's for grownups, Cady." Marlee sits up and swings her legs off the bed, stretching out her shoulders. "People who love each other."

"But we do love each other, don't we?" Cadence scooches up behind her, wrapping two skinny arms around her neck.

That's undeniable.

"I love you very much, sweetheart." Marlee glances at the clock on the bedside table, alarmed to

17

find the afternoon half lost already. "Oh! How long was I asleep? We have to go!"

"Go where?" Cadence rocks back on her heels, sulking as Marlee pulls away from her.

"Well, since you refused to sit for your fittings and have a dress made for you by your mother's modiste, we have to go out and buy you one. If we don't leave now, we'll never be back in time for dinner, and you know your parents don't like to be kept waiting."

"What do I need a new dress for?" Cadence makes no effort to move as Marlee retrieves a hairbrush from the dresser and pats the edge of the bed, beckoning her closer to have her wild chestnut locks tamed.

"You know what for, Cady." Marlee forces her to sit and have her hair brushed. "It's your birthday party on Friday."

"Don't call it that." Cadence scowls. "If it was my birthday party, I'd get to invite my friends and have ice cream cake."

"Your first debutante party, then," Marlee concedes.

"It's not a party of any kind," Cadence contends. "It's an auction." She folds her arms in protest. "You may as well just slap a price tag on me, leave me at the Sunday flea market, and hope for the best."

Unfortunately, she's right: it *is* like an auction.

A far cry from the sophisticated balls of the Victorian era, modern debutante affairs are much more sordid. The parents of an upper class coming-of-age girl will throw a party for the parents of all her potential suitors to attend. The parents meet the girl, quiz her on things of importance to them, determine whether or not they'd like to match her with one of their own offspring, then talk financials. Cadence will effectively be sold to the highest bidder.

"Oh, darling." Marlee kisses the top of her head. "I know you don't like being put on display, but this is an unavoidable part of growing up. I'm sure your parents will pick a wonderful match for you, so don't fret."

"How can you be so calm about this?" The frustration in Cadence's voice is laced with anger. How dare Marlee be so blasé!

If only she knew the truth.

Marlee is far from calm. She's been dreading this since the party was first announced. The thought of Cadence—her darling Cadence—being thrust into the arms of some strange boy she's never met and forced to accept him as her husband at the tender age of eighteen is both painful and horrifying. Not only that, but she won't even be around to witness it.

She won't be able to comfort Cadence in the days and weeks leading up to the marriage. She won't be able to counsel her on what to expect when she goes to live with her new husband. She won't get to offer her support on the morning of the ceremony. Why? Because her engagement, whenever that occurs, will spell the end of their time together. Too grown up for a nanny, she'll be assigned her own lady's maid instead.

Bye-bye, Marlee.

Hello, Adulthood.

At most, they have only a year or so left in each other's company, and Marlee intends to treasure every minute of it. Right now, she wants to hold Cadence firmly against her breast and confess how absolutely petrified she is of what the future might bring for them both ... but that would be unspeakably unprofessional. She can't admit that, nor confide how she sometimes cries into her pillow at night because of it. Instead, she must give Cadence courage.

"Everything will work out for the best." She wrangles Cadence's hair into a new, tidy ponytail and straightens her bangs. "I feel certain of it."

"How come this is all happening so soon?" Cadence's lipstick-smeared bottom lip trembles. "My cousin Julia didn't have her first debutante party until she was seventeen."

"Obviously your mother thinks you're already mature enough."

"Horseshit." Cadence clambers off the bed. "She just wants rid of me."

"Watch your mouth," Marlee reprimands her feebly.

"I'm not for sale, Marlee." Cadence is on the verge of tears, begging for reassurance. "I want to be with someone I love."

A natural but hopeless wish, Marlee thinks, loving how her name sounds as it tumbles off Cadence's tongue. Cadence's accent is thoroughly British, but she rolls the 'r' like her American father does, making it sound soft and warm: Marrrrrrlee. Like a kitten purring.

She wishes she had something comforting to say, but the sad truth is that Cadence has no choice in the matter. All decisions relating to her marriage and future life will be made by her parents, and for whatever reason, they've chosen to start the hunt early.

Summer holidays should be a time for fun and games, lazy mornings, and late nights. Cadence gets six whole weeks off school after finishing her GCSE examinations, but while other kids her age are going to water parks and funfairs, she's going to be worrying about whether or not she's about to be sold into someone else's bed. It's really not fair.

CADENCE HANGS ON MARLEE'S ARM, LEADING HER FROM one clothing store to another. She might not like the idea of the debutante party, but she's still a teenage girl: she likes shopping.

Marlee sticks with her wherever she wants to go, giving advice here and there about what sort of dress she should pick, and Cadence absorbs every word. Marlee's not simply telling her what might look good draped on her slender frame, but whether she realizes it or not, she's also spilling details about her own personal tastes in women's clothing. Cadence is gleaning valuable information.

"What if I don't even want to marry a boy?" she says suddenly, as a satin wedding gown in a bridal store window nabs her attention, reminding her of her impending fate. "Did anyone bother to think of that?"

Marlee hadn't, but she is now. Was that supposed to be a hint? What does it mean? Doesn't Cadence like boys? Is Cadence gay? Shit.

"Ooh!" Cadence practically dives into another store. "In here!"

Marlee follows her inside, somewhat stupefied. If Cadence isn't making a big deal out of it, then neither should she, but the thought of it is now stuck in her head like superglue.

Cadence. Gay. Really?

That loop keeps repeating, and she lets Cadence take the lead as they wander up and down seemingly endless clothing aisles, gathering an armful of possibilities. One of these is bound to be a hit. Surely?

She makes herself comfortable in a padded chair outside the changing rooms, resting her aching feet, waiting for Cadence to model for her—and Cadence takes great pleasure in doing so. Tirelessly, she tries on one dress after another, checking Marlee's reaction each time.

To the first one: "That's cute, darling."

Cute? Cadence pulls a face. Kittens and puppies are cute.

To the second: "You look adorable."

Ugh. That's even worse than cute! Little girls are adorable, and she definitely doesn't want to look like a little a girl. Especially not in front of Marlee.

The third and fourth receive similar feedback, but when she puts on the fifth—a black, asymmetrical dress with one lace sleeve, one bare shoulder, and a slanted hemline with a lace trim—she finally gets the result she's hoping for.

"You look ..." Marlee's voice trails off, her eyes roaming up and down.

Revelation number one: Holy shit, Cadence looks like a woman! The dress hugs her curves, accentuating every single one of them. As she bends to pick up a fallen clothes hanger, she points her ass in Marlee's direction and revelation number two hits: Cadence has an ass!

Aware that her mouth's stopped moving and no sounds are coming out, Marlee sighs deeply and smiles, words utterly failing her.

Cadence beams. "This is the one!"

No argument whatsoever from a very speechless Marlee. While she pays for it on Mister Ashlock's credit card—which she's authorized to use for any and all expenditures relating to the care and maintenance of Cadence—she spies her blossoming charge perusing the underwear aisle with casual interest.

The *sexy* underwear aisle.

Damn.

"What're you looking at?" Marlee meets her in the aisle, intending to coax her out of the store before anything catches her eye.

"Can I get some new underwear?" Cadence flicks through a rack of black lace push-up bras, trying to imagine what she'd look like in them.

"Whatever for?" Marlee tries to keep any and all thoughts of Cadence and underwear out of her head. "You have lots of underwear. We just replaced all your bras."

"Yeah, but it's all so ... kiddy." Cadence frowns forlornly. Right now, she's wearing plain white cotton undies. How dull and uninspiring.

"Kiddy?" Marlee questions.

Cadence holds up a rather lacy pair of knickers, demonstrating the very opposite. "I want something like this."

Marlee feels a flash of heat in her cheeks and tries to ignore it. "Don't you think you're a little young for this sort of thing?"

"I'm sixteen!"

"Almost, but not quite, and even then ..."

"Come on, Marlee." Cadence peers up at Marlee with moon-shaped, pleading eyes. "Don't you think I'd look pretty in them?"

Marlee starts to feel a little weak in the knee area, her stilted answer coming out in three broken, disjointed stages:

"That's not the point." It really isn't.

"You look pretty in everything." She really does.

"Your parents would kill me." They really would.

She dreads to think how it would look if they found sexy lingerie like that on the expenses receipts she has to submit at the end of every month.

"How are they ever going to know?" Cadence persists, completely ignorant of the financial hoops

Marlee has to jump through. "It's not like they do my laundry, or come into my room, or talk to me."

Oh, no. There's the impossible-to-ignore, emotional manipulation tactic. Marlee's vulnerable to it at the best of times, but now, with the image of Cadence wearing that dress still burning brightly in her mind, making her thoughts muddled, her recently awakened body waging war with all that remains of her common sense, she's positively helpless. Consequently, the words that end up leaving her lips next are disowned by her brain immediately.

"If you're going to get the knickers, you have to get the matching bra, too."

A tiny voice inside her head starts to scream, begging for her to stop. This is madness, she thinks, paying for both items on her personal credit card. In the entire two and a half years preceding this moment, the only things she's ever purchased on her own card to avoid being detected by her employers have been the occasional ice cream treat and one or two 18A movies.

"Please don't tell your parents," she begs Cadence needlessly as they leave the store.

As if she would.

Cadence loves the thought of keeping a secret with Marlee. Especially a sexy secret.

Quivering inside her push-up bra and gossamer knickers, Marlee hangs the debutante party dress inside the door of Cadence's closet, making sure it's perfectly flat so that it won't crease. It's a beautiful garment, made even more beautiful when Cadence's svelte body is filling it out.

Positively vibrating with a profound—albeit illicit—hunger for the surprisingly womanly body of her young charge, she presses a hand to her chest, trying to quell the rapidly beating heart within. Quivering? Over Cadence? How could she! Perhaps it's been too long since she's had a proper opportunity to satisfy certain physical desires. She needs a release.

Her last session with Rachel had been entirely one-sided, and without climax for either of them. She should've known there wouldn't really be enough time to accomplish anything significant in the short window they had, but she was exceptionally horny and willing to take whatever she could get. Maybe they'll have an opportunity for a do over tomorrow night, while Cadence is at her debutante party. She damn well hopes so. She can't take much more of this.

"What will you be wearing to the party?" Cadence asks, hanging her head off the side of the bed, looking at Marlee upside down.

"Oh, darling." Marlee closes the closet door, banishing the dress from sight. "I'm afraid I won't be attending with you."

Cadence flips over onto her front, rising to all fours. "Why not?!" Pure outrage.

"I wasn't invited to this one." Marlee approaches the bed, picking up items of strewn clothing along the way. "You know I don't always get to accompany you to family events."

"But you *do* always chaperone me at parties." Cadence pouts, rising to her knees at the foot of the bed, outstretching her arms for a cuddle.

Marlee tosses the clothes in the laundry basket and gives herself to Cadence, welcoming two spaghetti noodle arms around her neck. "This time, I think they want to make sure their esteemed guests see you as a woman, not as a child who still needs a nanny."

That gives Cadence some pause for thought.

Then, while keeping Marlee in a tight hold, "What do you see me as?"

25

Feeling the tickle of arousal stirring in her loins again, Marlee dare not say what she really feels. Sometimes, Cadence can behave in such a childlike manner: demanding to be tucked into bed at night, insisting on having her hair brushed, refusing to pick up after herself. But how much of that is genuine immaturity? Marlee's begun to harbor a suspicion that Cadence is deliberately clinging to old habits, simply to ensure that their relationship remains symbiotic.

It's different when she's not striving for attention. When she's not so anxious about losing her nanny's interest, she's an articulate, expressive young woman with a cheeky sense of humor and a captivating disposition. Little does she know that her increasing age and maturity makes her no less appealing to Marlee. In fact, it's proving to have quite the opposite effect.

As Marlee places her hands on Cadence's waist, she can't stop imagining her wearing that dress. There was no trace of a child earlier in the clothing store. Still, she can't admit that to her. Not outright. Instead, she settles for an answer that's both truthful and flattering, without being in any way unbefitting.

"I see you more like a young woman and less like a child every day."

Pleased enough to hear even such a small pinch of appreciation for her rocketing ascent into womanhood, Cadence pulls Marlee completely into the embrace and squeezes the air out of her lungs. "I like that."

"Me, too, sweetheart," Marlee whispers quietly, relishing the close contact.

"Are you sure you won't come to the party?" Cadence's voice is muffled against Marlee's neck, lips grazing skin.

"I can't, darling." Marlee suppresses a shiver. "Your parents don't want me there."

"But I want you to see me wearing that dress," Cadence grumbles. "I liked the way you looked at me when I modeled it for you."

Feeling a twinge of shame, Marlee regrets letting her eyes get so licentious. Was her attraction really that evident? Ugh. She should be utterly mortified. How could she look at Cadence as anything other than a soon-to-be sixteen-year-old girl? Mind you, it *is* only looking, and where's the harm in that? Convincing herself that she's in the clear, her mouth starts moving against the advice of her brain, words coming out unchecked.

"Why don't you wear it for me another night?" she suggests. "We'll both get dressed up and go out for dinner together. How does that sound?"

What is she saying?! It sounds inappropriately romantic, and Cadence is grinning.

"Perfect, Marlee." Cadence pulls back to look at her, cheeks pink with excitement. "I'd love to go out with you."

As she's swept into another hug, Marlee panics slightly. Did she just ask Cadence out on a date?

SEVENTEEN MINUTES. CADENCE HAS BEEN COUNTING, and that's precisely how long it's been since someone—anyone—has paid any attention to her at her birthday-cum-debutante party. At first, the parents of her potential suitors were all over her, asking her questions and making her spin in pointless circles. Now, they're huddled around her mother and father, asking them even more questions, most of which seem to be about money.

Bored and irritated, she slips away under the guise of needing the bathroom and goes on a hunt for Marlee, having no intention to return. After checking the most obvious places—her bedroom, the library, and the games room—she heads for the servants' quarters. Sometimes, when she's precluded from taking part in a family activity, or is otherwise surplus to requirements, Marlee will retreat here to drink tea and chat, or play cards with the domestics.

But not tonight.

Cadence skips down the stairs and pokes her head into the kitchen, nine different members of staff all swiftly abandoning their cards on the table to stand in her presence, which is a custom she's never particularly understood.

"May I help you, Miss Cadence?" The butler bends to speak to her in a rather condescending tone, as if she's still a small child.

"Where's Marlee?" she asks, scanning the table for a face that isn't there.

Without waiting for an answer, she darts back into the hallway and starts calling Marlee's name—loudly. This is much to the consternation of the housekeeper, who, at this hour, would very much like her to use her 'indoor voice' instead.

Cadence pays no heed, and eventually, she's rewarded with the appearance of a harried-looking Marlee, stumbling out from a housemaid's bedroom. Her hair is slightly tousled, her cheeks flushed, and she's struggling to fasten her open blouse, her bra-clad breasts spilling out from it.

"What is it, darling? What's wrong?"

Behind her, Rachel steps out looking equally disheveled.

"What's all the yelling?" She spots Cadence and immediately adopts a more appropriate stance, standing perfectly straight with her head slightly dipped. "I'm sorry, Miss. I didn't know it was you."

The apology means absolutely nothing. Marlee was in her room! Marlee was ...

Heart crushed, brain cells exploding, Cadence hightails it out of the servants' quarters.

"Shit!" Marlee puts her breasts away and makes chase, but Cadence disappears back into the closed-off ballroom before she can be caught.

"Buggering hell," Marlee mutters to herself, taking a seat on the bottom step of the main staircase, not sure what she should do next.

Should she wait? Should she make herself scarce? Time ticks by, and a full hour passes while she does nothing but chew down her fingernails. She hasn't yet come to a proper decision when the door to the ballroom swings open and Cadence's father strides through it, dragging Cadence along with him.

He's a tall man—over six feet—with thick gray hair and a goatee that's so pale it's almost white. In his early sixties, he's got plenty of age lines on his face, but he's still handsome. A former military man, he keeps himself in good shape, and uses those strong arms to throw Cadence across the foyer.

Marlee leaps to her feet, just in time to catch the flailing teen. "Darling!"

Mister Ashlock is so enraged he doesn't seem to hear the casual use of an inappropriate endearment, or bother to question why the nanny is there, in such a perfect position to catch his discarded daughter. He just starts shouting.

"Goddamnit, woman! Do we not pay you enough to teach her some good manners?!" He straightens the jacket of his formal dinner suit. "She's supposed to know how to behave like a lady, for god's sake. She's a disgrace to my name!"

Cadence reeks of booze.

Oh, lord. How much trouble could she get herself into in an hour? Plenty, apparently.

"Put her to bed," Mister Ashlock snaps. "I don't want to see her for the rest of the night."

Cadence is giggling, leaning against Marlee with all her weight, only held upright by Marlee's breasts and grappling hands.

"What did you do?" Marlee whines quietly as Mister Ashlock storms back into the ballroom. "You silly girl." She says that with not an ounce of anger, only love and concern.

Getting Cadence up the stairs to bed takes an inordinately long time, since putting one foot in front of the other seems to be more than her addled brain can cope with.

"I drank a lot of champagne," she slurs, resting her head on Marlee's shoulder. "Are we going to bed now?"

"*You're* going to bed. I'm going to bash my head against a brick wall for half an hour."

"Don't do that." Cadence tries to pat her cheek, misses, and slaps her neck. "You might hurt yourself."

Yeah, yeah, yeah. Marlee succeeds in getting Cadence into her bedroom, then into the bathroom adjoining it, and sits her down on the edge of the bathtub with a toothpaste slathered toothbrush in her hand. Despite missing her mouth the first time she tries to insert it, Cadence gets it between her lips on the second try, and Marlee retreats to the bedroom, folding and sorting clean laundry while she waits.

Was this her fault? Almost certainly, although Cadence probably didn't need much of a push toward finding a way to sabotage her first debutante party. Should she explain the situation to Cadence's parents in the morning? Probably, although that might get Rachel dismissed. Not that personal relationships between staff members are prohibited, but the Ashlocks have a rather nasty habit of venting their frustrations on anyone who seems to be distracting Cadence from her obligations, or causing her to underperform in some way.

Marlee's fairly certain they wouldn't actually fire *her*, although she did inadvertently ask their underage daughter out on a dinner date, which probably wouldn't help her case if the whole truth were to come spilling out.

"I'm done," Cadence calls from the bathroom.

"Come to bed, then," Marlee calls back, staying with the laundry.

Cadence drops her toothbrush in the sink, then staggers out and leans against her dresser, swooning and swaying at Marlee. "I think you're so beautiful."

Marlee, feeling guilty for being the cause of this, won't turn to look at her, unwilling to acknowledge her champagne-fuelled flirtation with a direct response. This is the second time in a row that she's had unsatisfactory, climax-lacking sex with Rachel, and she's on a short fuse.

"You're drunk," she sighs, dismissing the compliment.

Continuing to fold laundry, she hears a zipper, followed by the soft thud of fabric hitting the floor. Now she's *afraid* to turn around. Did Cadence just undress? Is she wearing her new underwear? Marlee mentally rebukes herself for letting the thought cross her mind. Who cares if she's wearing her new underwear? What difference does it make?

"Marlee," Cadence coos softly, urging her to turn around. "Look at me."

Her voice is so seductive. How is that possible? How can such a sexually naïve young girl be so damn seductive? Marlee closes her eyes and takes a deep breath. Can Cadence see how much she's struggling? Is she doing this on purpose?

With her heart thumping behind her ribcage, she twists to face her intoxicated, nearly naked teen, a small gasp of sincere appreciation escaping involuntarily at the sight of her.

"Do you like?" Cadence smirks.

She looks stunning. Her curves are so exquisite, from her slender shoulders to the peaks of her breasts, areolae just visible beyond the black lace cupping them, hard nipples tenting out the fabric slightly. Everything below her slim waist is more than perfect, too: her tiny bellybutton, flat stomach, the gentle sweep of her hips, and the small mound of her mons pubis at the apex of her thighs, dark pubic hair trapped behind the lace. And those legs! Long, milky, perfectly smooth legs. She's been shaving since she was thirteen.

Christ.

Marlee feels her body respond to Cadence's provocative form. She's entirely womanly, with a fully bloomed figure and young, silky, untouched flesh.

"Oh, heavens." Marlee looks away, pretending to be unaffected by the display. "The underwear looks lovely on you, darling. I knew that it would." She deliberately leaves all trace of emotion out of her voice.

Turning her back on Cadence, she busies herself fluffing pillows, picking stuffed toys off the bed, and pulling back the duvet, completely unaware of the emotional distress her casual disregard for Cadence's appearance has caused.

"Why don't you like me?" Cadence mopes, disappointed by the lack of attention, feeling slighted by Marlee's uninterested eyes.

"Oh, Cady." Marlee looks up, holding an armful of displaced teddy bears. "I *love* you. You must know how much I love you."

"But you don't think I'm pretty?"

Marlee's heart aches. So many times over the last year, she's been caught off-guard by Cadence's emerging womanhood. At some point, she'd become desperately aware of how the bony ass of a little girl had formed into the soft, round rump of an adolescent—a fact cemented in her mind while they were in the clothing store.

Likewise, the further development of her tiny breasts had come as a delightful surprise. On the first day of summer break this year, Cadence had taken advantage of the good weather and gone for a swim in the pool. Even though she's well on her way to adulthood, her parents still require that she be supervised at all times—something which neither she nor Marlee have ever complained about.

When she emerged from the clear, cool water, her bikini was clinging to two glorious mounds on her chest. She'd caught Marlee looking, they'd exchanged a smile, and Marlee cautioned herself against being so free with her eyes. But now Cadence is standing semi-naked in her bedroom, *demanding* that she look, feeling hurt when she doesn't.

"You're so beautiful, honey." Marlee scans Cadence from head to toe. "Why are you asking me these things?"

"What does Rachel have that I don't?" Cadence steps closer. "Does she please you more? Would you rather go out with her?" She sneers out the last word disdainfully.

"Oh, sweetheart." Marlee's heart feels as though it's about to rupture. "Are you jealous?"

That shouldn't be surprising at all. Outside of the time Cadence spends in school, or embroiled in extracurricular activities, they're together practically every waking hour of every day. Never has Marlee sought out any relationships that might take her away from the house. For one thing, she hasn't had the time. Tending to Cadence is a fulltime job, and she's been unreservedly devoted to caring for the child night and day, sneaking off to tend to her adult needs only when she was certain Cadence was preoccupied.

Until tonight.

Tonight, Cadence had seen something she'd never seen before.

"Do you love her more than me?" Cadence climbs onto the foot of the bed, creeping closer on her knees.

Marlee shakes her head, averting her eyes. "I don't love anyone more than I love you."

Kneeling, Cadence tugs the stuffed animals out of Marlee's hands and tosses them to the floor, positioning herself on the very edge of the bed.

"So why won't you look at me?" She coils her arms around Marlee's neck, rocking her hips forward, pressing their bodies together. "You're the reason I asked for lingerie. I thought if you saw me wearing something sexy, then you'd want me."

"Want you?" Marlee eyes Cadence's body tentatively, finding it hard to believe that the inexperienced teen actually understands the gravity of the words that are coming out of her mouth. "You have no idea how dangerously alluring you're becoming."

"Are you attracted to me, Marlee?"

She has a hopeful smirk on her face, her bottom lip pinched between her teeth. Dear god, she's so drunk. Her pupils are dilated, looking like saucers in her gleaming chocolate irises.

"Oh, darling." Marlee glides her hands around Cadence's tiny waist, so certain that she won't remember any of this in the morning. "Very."

Cadence giggles happily, swaying her hips, rubbing herself onto Marlee.

Marlee takes a deep breath. "Now you must get into bed." She pushes Cadence down onto the mattress, making her giggle again. "It's definitely past your bedtime."

"Will you lie with me?"

When she rolls onto her side, her breasts push together, forming a small 'v' of cleavage.

Marlee notices.

They've shared a bed together more times than either of them can count, ending so many nights with soft, warm cuddles.

Nevertheless, "I don't think so, sweetheart." Marlee pulls the covers over her. "Not tonight."

She perches on the side of the bed and bends to kiss Cadence goodnight—on the cheek, as she always does—but this time, the alcohol makes Cadence brave. A second before Marlee's lips make contact, she turns her head, pressing their lips together instead.

The peck lingers much longer than usual, until Marlee comes to her senses and pulls away from Cadence's soft pink mouth.

"Goodnight, my darling."

"Goodnight, my Marlee," Cadence mumbles sleepily. "I've waited so long for this."

"For what, love?"

No answer.

Cadence is already asleep.

CADENCE IS SNORING WHEN MARLEE BREEZES INTO HER bedroom and opens the drapes, morning sunlight streaming in. As a dazzling beam of light hits the bed and rouses Cadence, she grunts and covers her face with her pillow.

"Too early." Her voice is muffled beneath the pillow. "Come back tomorrow."

Marlee budges Cadence over and sits on the bed, reaching for her hand, kissing her fingers. "How're you feeling?"

"My head hurts."

"I'm not surprised." Marlee peels the pillow away from her, releasing her makeup smudged face to the horrors of daylight.

"Is my father very angry?" Cadence squints, putting up a hand to shield her eyes from the sun's frightful glare.

"I'm sure a sincere apology will go a long, long way." Marlee squeezes her hand. "And I'll explain that it was my fault. I'll say you walked in on—"

"No," Cadence doesn't wait for her to finish. "I don't want him to be cross with you as well. It's okay that he thinks I ruined my debutante party deliberately. It doesn't matter. I don't want him to know that I ... because you ..." She has difficulty articulating herself.

"I didn't mean to upset you last night, love." Marlee bends forward and runs her fingers through Cadence's tangled hair. "You shouldn't have seen—"

"Were you shagging Rachel?"

In the face of a momentary flare of panic, Marlee attempts to take that question in her stride. Contemplating the answer she's going to give, she leans across Cadence's chest and tilts her head, blocking out the sun. If they're going to have this conversation, they're damn well going to have it while looking at one another properly, not squinting.

In the end, though, she can't quite seem to find the right words. She nods slowly.

"Do you shag her a lot?" Cadence presses on.

Marlee indicates no with a sway of her head, although, technically, she supposes, the truth of that very much depends upon your definition of 'a lot'. To her, several times a week isn't really a lot, it's just enough to take the edge off. Anyway, this doesn't seem like a topic they should be discussing in any great detail.

As if reading her thoughts, Cadence asks her to clarify. "How often?"

"Only when I need—" Marlee stops herself. This is more than a sixteen-year-old girl in her care ought to hear. "Only sometimes," she says instead.

Feeling a little confined, overheating slightly with Marlee draped over her, Cadence wriggles herself up a few inches, her bare shoulders and a glimpse of the black lacy bra she slept in rising above the top of the duvet.

Marlee hopes the inquisition is over, but then ...

"Do you love her?"

This is getting more complicated by the minute, and Marlee doesn't know whether or not she should lie. Matters of love and sex have rarely been discussed between them, except to say that the latter should always be accompanied by the former.

Trying to think of the best way to phrase her answer, she strokes Cadence's cheek, her fingers making their way gradually lower. She stops first at Cadence's chin, then her neck, then her shoulder. One of the bra straps has slipped down over her arm, and Marlee trails her hand down to meet it.

"Love can be a very complicated thing, Cady." She hooks the wayward bra strap on the end of her forefinger. "It comes in lots of different forms."

"Like what?" Cadence angles her shoulder up, indicating that it would be perfectly acceptable for the strap to come off altogether, should Marlee wish it.

"Well, there's the kind of love I have for Rachel, which is that I love having sex with her." Marlee slips the strap back onto Cadence's shoulder, despite the unspoken offer. "And then there's the kind of love I have for you, which is that I love everything about you."

Cadence breaks into a smile. "Really?"

"Really." Marlee gives her an Eskimo kiss.

"So you still want to go out with me?"

Marlee falters. Every functioning brain cell she still has left recognizes that now would be the perfect opportunity to put a stop to this. Tell her no. Tell her it was a mistake; a misunderstanding; a momentary slip of reason. The trouble is, looking down at her hopeful face, her trusting eyes, and her beautiful smile, Marlee can't bring herself to disillusion or disappoint. Not only that, but—god help her—she doesn't want to. She capitulates.

"Yes," she says quietly, then adds a caveat. "Next time your parents are away."

Somehow, that makes it sound a whole lot worse. It implies there's something to hide, but where's the mischief in dinner? They've gone out for dinner together before. What's so different this time? Nothing, Marlee chooses to believe.

"Now get up and out of bed, else we'll both be late for breakfast." She slithers off the bed, pulling the duvet with her, quite proud of herself for handling Cadence's questions in a way that required no untruths, misdirection, or sudden information dumps which might've caused her sixteen-year-old brain to overload.

She's in such a good mood, she slaps Cadence's ass playfully as the groggy teen stumbles across the bedroom, rubbing crusties out of her eyes. The action elicits a squeal, which, in turn, brings Marlee's smile to a full-on grin. Damn, that was inappropriately flirtatious. She sucks her lower lip into her mouth, biting on it gently as she watches Cadence disappear into the bathroom.

Insanity, she reminds herself.

This is absolute insanity.

Humming a tune for no-one's pleasure but her own, she selects and lays out Cadence's clothes, from matching cotton underwear to what color scrunchie she's going to use to tie her hair in a French braid. Today feels like a French braid day.

Upon arriving in the breakfast room twenty minutes later, with matching braids—as requested by Cadence—they're greeted by two very somber Ashlocks. Apologies are exchanged all round: Cadence for acting out, stealing champagne, and getting shitfaced; Mister Ashlock for manhandling her out of the ballroom the way he did; and Missus Ashlock for not breastfeeding her as an infant, which is clearly the root of all this poor behavior.

Poor behavior? That's a bit much, Marlee thinks. It's practically a requirement for teens to help themselves to their parents' alcohol and get shitfaced at least once before they come of age, and that's been Cadence's only real indiscretion of late. Yet despite that, the Ashlocks are, as ever, exceptionally hard on their only child. They've always been slow to congratulate her achievements, but quick to pick up on her faults, and Missus Ashlock is by far the worst of the two.

A dour woman in her early forties, with jet black hair tied in a bun, thin lips, and a sickly pallor, Missus Ashlock—who is actually the second Missus Ashlock, on account of the first one failing to produce any offspring—appears to be perennially on the brink of depression. She never seemed to want Cadence. As soon as the cord was cut, the sweet bundle of pink skin was ushered into the arms of a nanny.

As a heavy stillness descends on the room, Marlee slips off one of her high-heeled shoes and rubs her foot over Cadence's calf, silently cheering her. It swells her heart to see Cadence's adorable pink lips curl upwards as she smiles into her cereal bowl.

The silence is only broken by the crinkle of Mister Ashlock's newspaper, and the rumple of Missus Ashlock's over-starched skirt as she crosses and uncrosses her beanpole legs.

"So what fascinating adventures do the two of you have planned for today?" Missus Ashlock finally asks, purely for the sake of asking rather than out of any real interest to know what the response might be.

"Can we go horseback riding?" Cadence asks Marlee, not her mother.

Marlee has to consider that for less than a second before arriving at an answer. Staring at Cadence's firm bum in skintight jodhpurs sounds like a perfect way to spend a few hours.

"We'll take a picnic," she suggests, building on the idea. "We'll go all the way down to the south field, by the lake. It's quiet there."

Quiet? Why was it necessary for it to be quiet? Quiet is just another word for secluded. Why had she felt the need to add that? Good god, if she could open up her cranium, remove her brain, beat some sense into it, then put it back, she would. Feeling self-conscious, she disengages her fondling foot. As she does, Cadence lets out a muted whimper of disappointment.

Shit, this is too much.

Excusing herself, she gets up from the table.

"Where are you going?" Cadence almost chokes on her cereal.

"Finish your breakfast. I'll get one of the stable hands to ready the horses."

Marlee winks at Cadence, curtseys politely to the Ashlocks, and glides out of the breakfast room. She notifies the stable hand first, then instructs the cook to prepare a picnic, changes into riding clothes, and meets Cadence by the barns half an hour later.

Yep. Skintight jodhpurs, knee high leather boots, and a fitted riding jacket—the perfect combination. Cadence thinks so, too, enjoying the rare sight of Marlee in something other than one of her many nanny outfits. There's only one horse waiting in the yard, though: Marlee's.

"Where's Bobo?" Cadence looks around, but doesn't see him.

"He needs to be re-shoed, honey. Do you want to take out your mother's horse? Or would you rather ride with me?"

Marlee's horse is a fine stallion, more than capable of taking an extra hundred and twenty-five pounds of weight, should Cadence be inclined to join her in the saddle.

And she is inclined.

Very inclined.

So they ride together to the south field, Cadence in front, Marlee behind, one arm around her waist. It's comfortable, close, and intimate without making Marlee feel guilty. As the sun rises higher in the sky, conversation flits from Cadence's exams—the teen being concerned that she flunked chemistry, but confident that she aced French—to their upcoming family mini-vacation. They'll be leaving a few days from now, and Cadence is excited.

Every year, she gets to pick the destination for a long weekend away during the summer, and this year, she's chosen Lymington: a little seaside village on the south coast. It's random, quite strange, and not at all the exotic hotspot that her parents were hoping for, but it's her decision to make and fair's fair.

On the way, there's laughter, a few giggles, more laughter, and by the time they reach the south field, the awkwardness of breakfast is forgotten, and Cadence's drunken antics from the night before are ancient history. In no hurry to get back to the house, Cadence suggests a swim in the lake, but Marlee refuses to skinny dip. Cadence threatens to throw her in fully clothed, but lacks the strength to follow through on the threat, and they collapse in giggles again.

Seeking respite from the midday heat, Marlee takes refuge in the shade of a tree and watches Cadence attempt to catch a butterfly.

She's growing up, there's no doubt about that, but she still has a playful spirit that Marlee hopes she never loses. She's energetic and vivacious, her eyes sparkling with a passion for adventure and discovery. She likes to climb trees, catch toads, and play in the dirt, and she's not prissy like a lot of other rich girls her age. She has no affectations, no insincerity, and not an ounce of malice. She's delightful.

The butterfly continues to evade her as she leaps and dives and flails, her cheeks becoming rosy and pink with the heat, and Marlee starts to get motherly.

"Come and sit down before you pass out." She taps the ground next to her. "It's much too hot for these antics."

On her way to the tree, Cadence peels off her tight-fitting riding jacket, revealing a sheer white camisole below. The fabric is so thin it's almost see-through, but Marlee doesn't let her eyes wander.

"Close your eyes," Cadence instructs, dropping to her knees beside Marlee. "I want to give you something."

Marlee looks suspicious, puckering her lips into a sexy pout before closing her beautifully painted lids. "Okay, Miss Cadence Ashlock, but if it's a worm, so help me I will—"

It's not a worm.

It's a lip kiss.

Warm, chaste, and tender. Like last night, but now completely sober.

When it's over, Marlee opens her gentle eyes. "What was that for?"

"Because I love you." Cadence traces a fingertip over Marlee's cherry red bottom lip. "And I like your lips. They're so soft."

Barely breathing, Marlee opens her mouth and captures Cadence's fingertip between her teeth, biting on her gently, making her gasp. As all sense and reason promptly evacuates her brain following the sensual kiss, she closes her lips around Cadence's finger and sucks on it, caressing it with her tongue.

While Cadence watches, mesmerized, Marlee takes her by the hand and sucks the whole finger into her mouth before pulling it out slowly, leaving a ring of red lipstick around the base.

"Wow," is all Cadence is able to articulate.

Like a fish out of water, she seems lost, not knowing what to say or do next. Her momentary inaction is more than enough to make Marlee regret behaving so recklessly.

"I'm sorry." She flushes with embarrassment, pulling Cadence's hand into her lap. "I don't know what I'm thinking lately. That was—"

"Amazing." Beaming like a ray of sunshine, Cadence recovers from her shock and snuggles against Marlee's chest, wriggling in between her legs.

Marlee hugs her arms around Cadence's lithe body, holding her tight.

"I love you," she whispers, kissing the side of her head. "More than I think I should."

Sitting there, perfectly content with Cadence in her embrace, Marlee makes a vow to herself: no more insanity. As of this moment, she's going to behave in a manner as befitting her position in the Ashlock household, and that's that. No more inappropriate touching, flirting, and certainly no more kissing—of any kind. She no longer trusts herself, and dare not even offer up any goodnight kisses for fear of losing her way.

It's just not safe.

NO MORE KISSES, MARLEE REPEATS TO HERSELF AS SHE waits for Cadence to finish brushing her teeth. She'll tuck her into bed, wish her goodnight, then leave. Just like that.

Her confidence is bolstered when Cadence emerges from the bathroom wearing blue fleece pajamas that have a fuzzy guinea pig pattern all over them. They're perfectly suitable nightclothes for a sixteen-year-old, and not in the least bit sexy.

Marlee's relieved.

She lets out Cadence's braid, dragging long fingers through her flowing chestnut tresses, loosening it up. Her hair's so thick and soft, like thousands of strands of silk.

"All right, into bed you get." She shoves Cadence gently, forcing temptation away.

She half expects the young girl to bring out the usual repertoire of protests—just five more minutes, read to me, lie with me, watch television with me till I fall asleep—but strangely, Cadence complies without a fuss. Either she's worn out from the day's activities, or she's eager to receive another kiss. If it's the latter, she's about to be sorely disappointed.

In short order, Marlee tucks her in, pats her arm fondly, and turns to leave, tendering nothing more than a faintly whispered, "Goodnight, darling."

"Wait." Cady holds her back, affronted. "Where's my kiss? We always kiss goodnight."

Nervous, and now highly conscious of the dangerously shifting dynamic of their relationship, Marlee sits down on the edge of the bed, deciding, in that moment, to treat Cadence precisely as she wishes to be treated: like an adult.

She starts by telling the truth.

"I'm afraid, darling."

Cadence frowns so deeply her eyes almost disappear. "Of kissing me?"

Marlee nods. "Earlier, in the south field, I ... I seem to be forgetting ... having some difficulty with ... trouble reconciling my ..." She takes a deep breath and starts again, trying to wrap her explanation up in language that Cadence will be able to grasp. "I'm expected to behave a certain way, just as you are, and lately, I've been misbehaving dreadfully."

"But I don't understand." Cadence huffs. "We've always kissed."

"Yes, but not like that."

A few seconds pass silently while Cadence digests Marlee's concerns, the cogs in her mind spinning and whirring at double pace.

Then, "So some kissing is okay, but not other kissing?"

"Exactly." Marlee smiles, pleased that she understands.

"Well, which is which?" Cadence puts on a practiced expression of naïve innocence, baiting the hook and tossing it in the water. "Will you show me?"

Marlee sees the hook dangling there—just as she had when Cadence touched her breast the other morning—but this time, much against her better judgment, she bites.

Bending forward, she starts by kissing the top of Cadence's head. "This is okay." Next, she kisses the side of her head. "So is this." Now her forehead. "And this." She moves to her cheek, giving her a peck just the same as their goodnight kisses always were. "Obviously this, and ..." She hesitates.

The next and last one is the most dangerous.

She hovers with her lips over Cadence's and nuzzles noses with her. "These are perfectly acceptable, but not ... anything ... more ..."

Pull away! A hundred voices in her head are all screaming the same thing, but her body fails to respond to any of them. She so badly wants Cadence to reel her in.

Closing her eyes, she endeavors to concentrate on cutting through the babble in her brain and having one clear thought. Everything's a jumble. Hand in your notice. Resign. Leave. Run. Kiss her. No, don't kiss her! Run! Cry. Find a therapist. Cry some more. Just one kiss. No! No kisses! Quit. Walk away.

Silence.

Her mind is suddenly blank. There are no thoughts at all, just the unbelievably erotic sensation of Cadence's lips pressed against hers. Had she initiated the kiss? Had she leant closer? Who moved against who? Checking to see, she feels for the pillow, finding Cadence's head raised off it. Cadence had come to her!

It lingers much too long.

She brings her hand up to cradle the back of Cadence's head and reciprocates the kiss, pinching Cadence's lips between her own as she pushes the exuberant teen down into the pillow ... where she finally breaks away. Afterward, she opens her eyes and finds young Cadence elated, her lips tinged with traces of red lipstick.

"That was a nice kiss." Cadence grins. "Even better than this afternoon. And last night."

Marlee sinks beneath several layers of shame, one piling right on top of the other, coming in waves until she feels as though she's drowning in guilt. "You remember last night?"

Cadence nods happily. "Our first lip kiss."

Oh, it was so much more than that, Marlee recalls. She'd confessed her attraction. Why had she done that? Those words should never have been spoken.

She feels dizzy.

This has to stop.

Oblivious to Marlee's ongoing inner turmoil, Cadence is still grinning. "So can every kiss be like this from now on? I don't want to go back to boring kisses."

Marlee strokes Cadence's cheek, her heart swelling and aching in equal measure.

"We have to be so careful, darling. We're getting much too close."

Cadence's grin widens. "You didn't say no."

She should, but can't.

She bids Cadence a swift goodnight, then slips through the cheater door into her own room and leans up against it, breathing heavily. She considers locking it for the first time ever, but can't bring herself to do it. If Cadence has nightmares ... fuck.

Her chest feels impossibly tight, her clothing so constricting. She unfastens the first few buttons of her blouse, giving herself more imaginary breathing room, and fans her face, trying to lower her temperature.

It's so damn hot in here.

She crosses the room and opens the window, letting a blast of cool night air in, inhaling it like she's oxygen deprived. Exhausted, her brain swimming with a flurry of conflicting thoughts—her love for Cadence, her guilt for loving Cadence; her love, her guilt; love, guilt—she flops down onto the bed.

Her cunt is throbbing.

"Oh, my god." She covers her face with her hands, willing her body to calm.

It doesn't work.

Cadence's kisses are so thrilling, her lips so delicious.

"Damn it."

Closing her eyes, Marlee pulls up her skirt and reaches beneath, slipping a hand inside her underwear, finding herself absolutely drenched. She starts to moan, but quickly stifles it. What would Cadence think if she could hear? Would she know what the noises meant? Would she know she was the cause? Losing control, Marlee whines, desperate to feel some kind of release. She can't even hear herself; her voice is drowned out by the echo of her heartbeat in her ears.

She hopes she's being quiet.

She hopes she's being discreet.

Or does she? Fuck it. She groans loudly, touching herself to a fantasy of her sixteen-year-old charge—a girl who's completely out of bounds.

Her kisses. Her caresses. More.

Oh, shit, so much more.

MARLEE WAKES UP FIVE MINUTES BEFORE HER ALARM, having slept soundly and deeply after bringing herself to an incredibly intense climax right before bed. Mmm, Cadence. Sweet, beautiful Cadence. Innocent, delicate, off-limits Cadence.

Damnit.

Cadence.

Feeling a familiar sensation of warmth behind her, she rolls over. Sure enough, Cadence is lying there next to her, sleeping comfortably.

"Darling." Marlee rouses her by squeezing her shoulder.

Cadence stirs and stretches, rolling onto her back. "What time is it?"

"Almost nine." Marlee slides a hand over her stomach, kissing the side of her head. "What are you doing in my bed? Did you have a bad dream?"

"No." Cadence smiles sweetly. "I just wanted to sleep with you."

Marlee's chest aches again. She wonders if Cadence has any idea what powerful, adult feelings she's provoking. How could she? She's only sixteen!

As much as she'd like to stay exactly where she is, Marlee drags herself away and gets out of bed. "You're really getting too old for this, Cadence."

Some of Cadence's happiness fades. Marlee only ever uses her full name when she's serious about something. Propping herself up on her elbows, she watches Marlee cross to the bathroom and start brushing her honey-colored hair.

She's wearing a black silk negligee, the smooth fabric hugging her feminine body, hinting at the perfection hidden beneath. She's the most shapely woman Cadence has ever seen, her breasts full and round, her hips curvaceous, her ass ... yum.

"Why?" she asks at last. "Why am I too old to sleep in your bed?"

"You're maturing." Marlee pads barefoot back to the bed and pushes Cadence upright, sitting behind her to brush her long, dark locks. "You're a young woman, not a little girl."

"Isn't that better?"

Better? Marlee's brushing falters for an almost imperceptible half-second. In what way could that be better? She's not going to ask. Instead, she changes the subject.

"Are you excited for the vacation you picked? We leave the day after tomorrow."

"It's going to be the best vacation ever!" Cadence smirks to herself. "No talk of stupid piano lessons and debutante parties."

"I couldn't agree more, but why ever did you choose Lymington? It's so obscure, and it's so close to ... well, it's just so close really. We're barely leaving the bloody county, never mind the country."

Cadence shrugs. "I opened a map and poked my finger at it."

Marlee isn't surprised. That really does sound like something Cadence would do. Interrupted by a knock at the door, she leaves Cadence to brush out the rest of her hair and answers the door to find one of the junior maids standing there with an envelope in her hands.

"Letter for you, Miss Meeks." She hands it over, curtseys, and scurries off.

Marlee doesn't even have a chance to say thank you before the young girl disappears into a servants' stairwell. She's not meant to be in this wing of the house. What she just did probably felt like breaking the law, and reeks of a cruel trick played on her by the more senior domestics who take great pleasure in causing the humiliation of the junior staff members by getting them into trouble.

Anyway, more curious about the letter—which is addressed simply to Marlee and clearly came from within the house—than she is about downstairs games, she slices the handwritten envelope open with her thumbnail and pulls out a watermarked piece of notepaper.

It's from the Ashlocks, who are writing to inform her that they've been called away to London on urgent business and won't be joining her and Cadence in Lymington. The whole thing is brief, impersonal, and just another example of the ugly way they treat their daughter. But what else can you expect from two people who only had a child as a means to acquire more wealth? Love never had anything to do with it.

"What is it?" Cadence asks from the bed.

"Your mother and father have gone to London." Marlee tears the worthless note in half and drops it into a wastebasket. "They won't be coming with us to Lymington."

"Really?" Cadence's lips curve upward. "So it's going to be just the two of us?"

"Yes, my darling."

Cadence leaps up and flings her arms around Marlee. "I can't wait! I'm going to start packing!" She runs into her bedroom. "And I'm bringing the dress!"

Marlee cracks a smile, feeling grateful for never having to worry about Cadence getting upset over being abandoned by her parents. By her own admission, she stopped caring when she was five years old and they sent a similar letter saying they wouldn't be attending her birthday party. Heartless bastards.

Forcing all thoughts of the rotten Ashlocks out of her mind, Marlee gets dressed and steals the opportunity to catch up on some laundry while Cadence is busy deciding how many different pairs of jeans she ought to pack. That should take a while.

The laundry room is located in the servants' quarters, next to the kitchen and scullery. Updated and fitted with modern washing and drying machines—three of each, to cope with heavy laundry days—the only thing left of any historical significance here is the original tiled floor, which Marlee is always nervous to walk on, afraid that her stiletto heels will chip a tile, or get wedged in between them.

She's always insisted upon doing Cadence's laundry. It's one of those chores that, in her view, happens to fit naturally under the umbrella of caring for Cadence, even though there's a whole fleet of housemaids who would be more than willing to do it at her request.

It just seems so personal, and she doesn't feel right allowing the other domestics to handle Cadence's intimates. She feels like she's preserving Cadence's privacy and dignity—and now their secrets, too. In the laundry basket, she finds the black lacy knickers. If anyone else saw these ... geez. It doesn't bear thinking about.

Getting ready to toss them into one of the washing machines, she notices some white staining on the gusset. Shit. Was Cadence aroused the other night? Was she horny? Did she come? Curious, Marlee brings the knickers to her face, smelling Cadence's scent.

Damn.

"Did you just smell my dirty undies?"

Cadence's voice makes Marlee jump.

"No!" Shocked and embarrassed, she bundles them into the machine, banishing them from sight. "I certainly did not."

"Yes, you did! I saw you." Cadence hops up onto a dryer, grinning. "It's okay. I don't mind. Do you like the way I smell?"

"Darling, don't ask me that." Marlee finishes loading the machine.

"Why not?"

"It's inappropriate."

"More inappropriate than you smelling my intimates?"

Marlee can't argue with that. She sets the machine to spin, doing anything she can to avoid having to make eye contact.

"You have the aroma of a woman." She tries to explicate her behavior. "It surprised me, that's all. You're definitely not a child anymore."

"So you liked it?"

"Yes," Marlee admits tentatively. "You smell nice." She looks up at Cadence finally. "Now please keep your voice down, and let's change the subject."

"Fine." Cadence is still grinning. "Can we go shopping again? I think I'd like to buy more knickers."

MARLEE STARTS TO SERIOUSLY CONSIDER THE possibility that she might be losing her mind. She tries to recall if anyone in her family has ever been committed, or suffered a breakdown, or developed early onset dementia of some kind.

She can't think of anything significant. Her uncle Bob always seemed a bit off, but she'd been told that was only because he'd been deprived of oxygen at birth. Anyway, apart from lusting after a teenage girl, she feels perfectly mentally competent, and she's not quite old enough to be having a mid-life crisis. So what is this? Some kind of hormone imbalance? She rules out the possibility of early menopause for two reasons: one, a drop in hormones should make her less sexually erratic, not more so; and two, she still gets a period every twenty-eight days like clockwork, so there's not likely to be anything abnormal going on down there.

Maybe she has too much estrogen. Is that a thing? Does that make you rampantly horny for no apparent reason? Even now, her body's aching for something. She's sitting across the table from Cadence in a small café, bags of lingerie at her feet. They're surrounded by sane, rational people who would all think she'd gone round the sodding twist if they knew what an exorbitant amount of money she'd just spent on lingerie for a sixteen-year-old.

This isn't normal.

In fact, this is spiraling so far out of the realm of normal that it's making her a little nauseous. She picks up her latte to take a sip and glances at Cadence, wondering what she's thinking. For the last five minutes, she's been staring intently at a kissing couple in the corner of the room.

Probably in their early twenties, the couple have their tongues so far down each other's throats it's a wonder they can still breathe. Every now and again, the boy puts his hand on the girl's thigh, and she responds by pushing him back down toward her knee. At least one person here still has some sense of decency.

What could be on Cadence's mind, though? She's never spoken about boys, except to suggest that she might not want to marry one. She's never confided in Marlee about school crushes, or boyfriends, or going on dates. She's never been on a date. Has she ever been asked? Why the secrecy? Perhaps there's nothing to hide. Perhaps she's still too young. After all, she's been very sheltered.

At the request of the Ashlocks, Marlee had never educated Cadence in such things. They didn't want their daughter encouraged to date, to explore, or to become worldly in that way. The less thought given to the matter the better, they'd said, since her personal feelings aren't going to be taken into consideration anyway.

On the rare occasions that Cadence asks for specifics on certain topics, Marlee never lies, but Cadence seems to have little interest in romantic pursuits. Still, she's only sixteen, Marlee reminds herself. There's plenty of time for that to develop.

As the kissing couple finally break for air, Cadence turns back to the table and to her cup of steaming hot chocolate, thinking deeply before asking:

"Will you kiss me like that?"

Marlee coughs and wheezes, choking on her latte, some of the hot liquid getting caught in her windpipe. "Why in the world would you ask me such a thing?"

"Because I like it when our lips touch," she says matter-of-factly. "Do you?"

Marlee sets her cup down and stares into the bottom of her drink. "Far too much."

She looks saddened, and Cadence can't fathom why.

"What do you mean?"

"You're only sixteen, Cady." Marlee sounds deeply apologetic. "It wouldn't be proper for me to kiss you like that. Do you understand? It's against the law."

"No, it's not." Cadence scowls, angered by the suggestion. "I'm old enough now. I—"

"Not for me," Marlee cuts her protest short. "I'm your nanny. The rules are different."

Cadence, utterly flummoxed by this unforeseen stumbling block, is rendered temporarily silent, her disappointment palpable.

Then, "How different?"

"Eighteen," Marlee answers with a sigh. "As long as I'm still your nanny, you have to be eighteen."

"But we love each other," Cadence counters.

Oh, how her view of the world is so adorably simplistic.

"Darling"—Marlee reaches for Cadence's hand on the table—"I could get in a lot of trouble for kissing you that way. Besides anything else, do you know how old I am?"

Cadence shakes her head, sipping her drink.

"I'm thirty-three. I'm more than twice your age." She wishes that weren't true. "For god's sake, I'm old enough to be your mother."

Cadence sets her cup down so forcefully it almost cracks the saucer. "If you don't want to give me kisses that way, just say so. Don't make any more excuses." She looks crestfallen, her eyes full of tears.

Marlee is heartbroken. "Sweetheart, I would love to kiss you that deeply. I really would." She weaves her fingers between Cadence's. "It hurts me how much

I want to love you that way, but I just can't. Please try to understand."

It's clear that Cadence really doesn't understand—or doesn't want to. She barely says a word for the rest of the day, and things are so strained between them that, when it comes to bedtime, Marlee isn't even sure if the sulking teen wants to be tucked in.

Collecting Cadence's laundry from the dryer, she uses its delivery as thinly veiled subterfuge for entering the bedroom, and starts putting things away quietly while Cadence brushes her teeth. With a few minutes to think, she decides to let Cadence be the one to break the stalemate if she wants to, and if not, then maybe that wouldn't be so bad. A cooling off period might do them both some good.

But that's not the way things play out.

Cadence returns from the bathroom, exploiting her peripheral vision to watch Marlee remove the last item from the laundry basket, waiting for her to speak first. When that doesn't happen—and as soon as she realizes Marlee intends to leave without saying a word—she finally calls out to her, breaking the silence.

"Will you tuck me in?"

Marlee's more relieved than she thought she'd be to hear her ask. "Of course I will, darling. I wasn't sure if you'd want me to."

She abandons the laundry basket on the floor and settles Cadence into bed, pulling the duvet up around her shoulders before perching on the edge to say goodnight.

"Sleep well, my love." She moves stray hair away from Cadence's eyes, brushing her bangs aside, smiling fondly at her, pleased not to be fighting anymore.

"I still want a goodnight kiss," Cadence reminds her.

As if Marlee could forget. Hoping to get their relationship back on the right track, she bends to kiss Cadence's cheek ... but Cadence evades her.

"Not that kind," she insists. "It has to be lips, else I'll still be cross with you."

"Cadence ..." Marlee frowns disapprovingly.

"Marlee."

At the unexpected sound of her name, Marlee feels a surge of arousal between her legs. How is that possible? How can one word do that?

"Say my name again," she begs.

"Marrrrrrlee," Cadence whispers, drawing it out. "I love you."

That almost does the trick. Marlee rolls her tongue over her lips, moistening them.

"Marlee," Cadence tries again, determined to win this battle of wills. "I want you to kiss me."

With a whimper, Marlee capitulates. Hoisting the white flag of surrender, she bends forward and brings her lips to Cadence's, stealing another illicit, closed-mouth kiss from her charge—but Cadence isn't sated by that. When their mouths touch—the tentative bumping of lips quickly evolving into an erotic clinch— she flicks her tongue against Marlee's lips.

This daring escalation of intimacy manages to elicit a soft, involuntary murmur from Marlee, but nothing comes of it. Sticking to her guns, Marlee pulls back and sits up, retreating from the kiss entirely.

"What did I tell you about kissing me like that?" The disapproving frown returns.

"But it's so unfair," Cadence protests. "It's only a kiss. Why shouldn't we be allowed to kiss?"

Sensing Marlee's lingering weakness—positively pouncing on her inability to say no—Cadence sits up and moves toward her. Swiftly initiating another kiss, she teases Marlee's lips apart with her tongue, and shudders with pleasure when she feels Marlee give in to her. Win!

Eyes closed, Marlee lets Cadence's tongue find hers, murmuring again as Cadence invades her mouth, kissing her so deeply. It's adult in every way, their lips locked together, their tongues caressing, probing, and exploring, and she whines with disappointment when it breaks.

Cadence flops against the bed. "That was perfect. Just like I imagined it would be." She grins up at Marlee from the pillow. "I like kissing you a lot."

Marlee licks her lips, tasting Cadence's toothpaste, astounded by her proficiency. "Wherever did you learn to kiss like that? That was so grown up."

"I practiced." Cadence beams proudly. "I wanted to be good for you. I didn't want you to think I was terrible."

That's the third time Cadence has insinuated harboring a long-held desire for her nanny, and the sudden realization that she's been planning this for a while has Marlee flooding between her legs again, her body longing for so much more than a kiss.

"Darling, how long have you felt this way?"

Cadence shrugs. "Since I was thirteen," she reveals candidly. "I stopped having nightmares when I was eleven, you know. Long before you became my nanny. All those times I climbed into bed with you, I was only pretending."

"Why?" Marlee's voice is softer than a whisper.

"I wanted to be closer to you. I like it when you hold me. Feels so safe and warm."

Marlee cups Cadence's cheek, silently admiring her.

"I like the way you look at me, too," Cadence adds, reveling in Marlee's loving gaze.

"How do I look at you?"

"Like there's only me in the world."

After playing it out in her head several times, Marlee leans forward and kisses Cadence again, seeking out her tongue deliberately and confidently, causing Cadence to mewl with surprised delight.

It feels much too good.

Forcing herself to stop before she gets caught up in the moment, Marlee breaks her lips free. "I love you," she whispers. "But I have to go."

Cadence nods, not expecting anything more.

THE NEXT MORNING, CADENCE WAKES HERSELF UP AND gets dressed entirely on her own for the first time since ... well, possibly ever. She's in a hurry to get the day started, and to spend as much of it as possible with Marlee.

Too eager to wait for Marlee to come to her, she dashes into Marlee's room with the intention of diving onto the bed and waking her up, but not only is the bed empty, it's already been made. Do the housemaids usually see to the beds this early? She shrugs. How the hell would she know? Marlee's the only one who makes her bed now.

Thinking Marlee must've risen extra early for breakfast, Cadence heads for the morning room.

Still no Marlee.

There's only one other place Cadence can think she might be, so she skips down the stairs to the servants' quarters and starts calling out her name.

"Not this again," the housekeeper mutters from the kitchen, trying to enjoy a peaceful cup of tea and a slice of toast.

Cadence looks here, there, and everywhere, and is about to give up and try somewhere else in the house when the back door swings open and Marlee enters— with Rachel. The two are laughing and carefree, Marlee with a basket of blackberries in her arms, but the laughter dies on their lips when they realize Cadence is standing there.

"Good morning, Miss." Rachel dips her head and curtseys.

She doesn't see what happens next, but Marlee does. It's as though Cadence's heart is shattering right in front of her. She looks crushed, tears welling in her eyes, her cheeks colored with envious fury, hurt beyond all measure.

"Oh, Cady." Marlee takes a step toward her. "No, no, no. This isn't—"

Her words fall on deaf ears.

For the second time in under a week, Cadence bursts into tears and runs off.

"Goddamnit." Marlee thrusts the basket of berries at Rachel. "Here, take these."

Rachel pulls a face. "What was all that about?"

Marlee offers up nothing elucidating and takes off after Cadence, chasing her through the house until she finally catches her in a restricted area on the top floor: the games room. Complete with a pool table, darts board, video game system, ping pong table, poker table, and all the board games you could imagine, it caters to almost every need. Including, apparently, teenage girls who just want somewhere quiet to hide and cry.

Off limits to most of the domestics—for fear that they might take to abusing the room for their own fun— it's a haven that's seldom used by anyone but Cadence and the occasional guests she invites. Right now, she's using it to sob into an enormous beanbag.

In the doorway, Marlee presses a hand over her chest, pausing to catch her breath.

"Do you have any idea how difficult it is to run in this outfit?" She's almost hyperventilating. "Or these stupid shoes." She kicks off her high heels. "It's a deep expression of my love that I even made it up here."

"Go away." Cadence's voice is muffled against the beanbag.

Marlee won't do any such thing. She gathers up her skirt and attempts to lower herself gracefully onto the beanbag, failing miserably. Heavier than Cadence, when she loses her balance and tumbles down onto it, Cadence's side of the beanbag rises up and sends her rolling backwards, their bodies colliding.

"Ooh, that's better." Marlee pulls her close, kissing the top of her head.

"Stop it!" Cadence wriggles away from her. "You had sex with Rachel again!"

"No, sweetheart. I didn't."

Cadence is behaving like a jealous lover, and although Marlee hates to see her this upset, the fact that she could even *get* this upset over witnessing a perceived act of infidelity moves her deeply. Too deeply. The thought of having Cadence as a lover is surprisingly, dangerously intoxicating.

"Yes, you did!" Cadence maintains the belief, struggling to get to her feet.

"Darling, don't go." Marlee looks up from the beanbag, skirt bunched around her thighs, her long legs exposed all the way up to the top of her stockings. "Stay here with me."

If Cadence weren't so upset right now, she'd think Marlee was the most beautiful and alluring creature she's ever seen. But she *is* upset, and she feels betrayed.

"I thought"—she chokes for breath—"after last night ... you kissed me ..." More sniffles. "I thought you wanted me."

"I *do* want you."

Marlee puts so much emotion into those words that the heartfelt confession stuns both of them. Marlee is alarmed by how easily the words roll off her tongue— without any hesitation or reservation—and Cadence is amazed by how they make her feel. As her tears dry up, something very different happens between her legs, her body aching with a desire she can't quite name.

Meanwhile, Marlee stretches out on the beanbag. She has one arm resting across her stomach, the other above her head, and her back is slightly arched, pushing out her chest.

Cadence watches intently. "Are you flirting with me, Marlee?"

Marlee slightly crooks one of her legs, causing her skirt to ride up an inch or two higher, unveiling a splash of pale thigh. "I think I might be."

Before Marlee has a chance to change her mind—as if there's any likelihood of that—Cadence drops back down onto the beanbag, melting into her arms.

"Do you really want me?"

Since actions speak louder than words, and Marlee hasn't got a clue what to say anyway, she leans forward and runs her tongue over Cadence's lips, moistening them, teasing them apart. When Cadence is ready to be kissed, Marlee cradles her neck and lays a passionate lip-lock on her.

No encouragement needed.

No coercion.

No trickery.

"Kissing you feels so divine," she confesses when the kiss breaks, immediately scooping Cadence's willowy body into an embrace. "I love your mouth."

They kiss again, all self-restraint lost. They're a bundle of whimpers and whines, tongues moving this way and that, lips pressed tightly together, and several minutes go by before they stop for a much needed breath of air.

"Ask," Marlee urges Cadence then. "Don't let it fester between us."

Not entirely sure that she really wants to hear the answer, Cadence's voice is hushed and low. "What were you doing with Rachel?"

"She spends a lot of time in the gardens, and she knows the very best places to pick wild berries. Did you not see the basket I was carrying?"

Nope. She'd been too busy remembering the sight of Marlee with an open blouse and tousled hair, imagining so many heartbreaking things.

"I didn't expect you to be up this early," Marlee continues. "I was picking berries with her because I was going to make you breakfast in bed. I still can if you want me to. It's never too late to go back to bed."

What the hell does that mean? Marlee has no idea. The sensible part of her brain shut off the instant she decided to lounge all over the beanbag like a cat in heat, flaunting her thighs.

Speaking of her thighs, Cadence's eyes are wandering, and Marlee wonders how brave she might be. Will she try to touch? Does she want to? A few seconds of quiet appreciation pass, then Marlee gets her answer: Cadence lunges at her with another kiss. In the midst of the lip-lock, she feels heat and pressure on her knee, moving slowly upward.

Cadence's hand, creeping up, up, up ...

"Careful." Marlee stops her from getting above the stocking. "Not too much."

"Why not?" Cadence asks, not giving Marlee any time to compose an answer. "Will you take your clothes off for me?"

"What?" Marlee mouths the word, hardly any sound coming out.

"Don't get me wrong, your nanny outfits are amazing." Cadence admires Marlee's form. "They're sexy, you look gorgeous in them, and I love staring at your cleavage, but my parents aren't home, and I think we should take advantage of that."

"Really?" Marlee raises an eyebrow, more shocked than she is excited.

Cadence can't possibly be thinking about sex. Can she? Regardless, all the blood in Marlee's body rushes straight between her legs.

"Uh-huh." Cadence fingers the bust of Marlee's blouse, undoing the first button, her fingers brushing against Marlee's breasts. "I want you to wear something casual today, and I want you to let your hair down. I like it that way."

Deeply relieved, and feeling foolish for thinking Cadence could've meant anything more, Marlee chuckles. "You want me to *change* my clothes, not take them off."

"Oh, I'm sorry." Cadence feigns sincerity. "Was I not clear?"

"You're such a tease." Marlee slaps the teen's thigh lightly.

"Of course, if you *do* want to take your clothes off for me ..." Cadence throws the thought out there, letting Marlee decide how seriously it should be taken.

"Stop it." Marlee tugs the hem of her skirt down a few inches. "You're a bad influence."

Following one more kiss, they cuddle together, slipping into a comfortable silence. Marlee almost dozes off, until Cadence's voice draws her back from the brink of unconsciousness.

"Marlee?"

"Mm-hmm."

"Are we going to have sex?"

All of a sudden, Marlee's wide awake. Cadence *is* thinking about sex!

"What do you mean, darling?" She needs some clarification. "Ever? Or right now?"

One of Cadence's shoulders rises and falls briefly. "Soon, I guess."

"No, my love." Marlee squeezes her tightly. "You're much too young."

Expecting a series of increasingly difficult to answer follow-up questions, Marlee's pleasantly surprised when Cadence says nothing, seemingly content with the facts as they are.

Phew.

Chapter Ten

THE REST OF THE DAY IS FILLED WITH STOLEN SMOOCHES, inside the house and out. First, they change into riding clothes and head back to the south field, kissing beneath the tree. Long, drawn out kisses, with plenty of snuggles to boot. Then, Cadence urges Marlee out of her restrictive nanny's clothing and into casual wear—jeans, and a white camisole with a loose summer shirt buttoned over it—and they play kiss chase in the house, keeping to areas where access by the rest of the domestic staff is limited.

They'd never be able to do this if the Ashlocks were home. They simply wouldn't dare.

By the time evening falls, Marlee is starting to feel a lot less guilty about her blossoming feelings for Cadence. It's only kissing, after all. Where's the harm?

Exhausted, completely worn out by much younger and much more athletic Cadence, she collapses on the sofa in the games room.

"I can't run anymore," she flatly declares. "You win."

"Are you saying you can't keep up with me?" Cadence teases, resting on top of her. "Am I too much for you?"

"God, yes." Marlee wraps her arms around the enthusiastic teen. "You're much too much for me, darling. For the sake of my health, I should probably swear off you, like I have wine and chocolate. Both of those things get me into trouble, just like you do."

"Fine. I'll leave, then," Cadence bluffs, making a weak effort to get off the sofa.

Determined not to let her go, a playful Marlee grabs at her waist and hips, holding her back, which is all fun and games until one of her hands ends up pressed completely over one of Cadence's breasts. Upon feeling the delightful, mound beneath her palm, she withdraws.

"I'm sorry. I didn't mean to—"

"No, it's okay." Cadence wriggles closer, lying with her back against Marlee's chest. "You can touch me there. I want you to."

Marlee tries to make time stop. When did this happen? When did Cadence become such a sexual being? Since when has she longed to be touched?

She strokes Cadence's waist and ribs, not daring to move her hands any higher. Glancing down, she can see Cadence's breasts outlined in her t-shirt, bulging out from her chest, stretching the fabric tight. They're modestly-sized, but the t-shirt is old and not fitted to accommodate her changing body.

She finds herself wondering what Cadence's nipples feel like. Are they big? Small? She imagines them delicate and pink, the surrounding areolae sensitive, and swollen with the need to be touched, kissed, sucked.

Her own breasts start to react, her nipples visibly erect. Thank god Cadence can't see. Moreover, thank god female arousal is easier to conceal than a man's! She can only imagine how difficult it would be to lie here with Cadence sprawled all over her, an erection throbbing in her crotch. Cadence would be able to see it, feel it, and touch it if she wanted to. Her attraction would be prominent and undeniable. As it is instead, at least she can pretend she's not so affected, not so wet, and not so damn horny.

Unfortunately, being able to hide her excitement does nothing to lessen it, and Cadence isn't about to let her off the hook just because there's no tangible proof of her arousal.

"Are you afraid again?" she asks, wondering why she's yet to feel Marlee's soft hands exploring her aching chest.

"I'm fucking petrified," Marlee answers without really thinking, quickly wondering if that's the first time Cadence has ever heard her curse like that.

If it is, she doesn't comment on it.

"Here." She takes Marlee's hands and places them on her chest. "Touch."

Marlee bites her tongue, suppressing a moan; Cadence is so caressable.

"Oh, Cady," she purrs, cupping two perfectly developed breasts. "What're you doing to me?"

Weak with lust, she fondles Cadence through the layers of clothing, finding a pair of tiny nipples, feeling them stiffen in response to her touch.

The pleasure is twofold. Firstly, there's the simple sexual thrill of touching her—the same thrill she would get from touching any woman. Secondly, there's the undeniable exhilaration of possibly being the first one—the *only* one—to experience this with her.

But what is this leading to? Sex with Cadence? Unthinkable! With that terrifying thought in mind, despite Cadence writhing around on her like a little worm, basking in all the new sensations that are rippling through her body, Marlee puts an end to it.

"I have to stop, darling." She slides her hands back down to Cadence's waist.

"Why?"

"The feelings you evoke in me are too intense." She kisses the side of Cadence's head several times in quick succession, tempted to press lips to neck, but resisting. "If we keep going like this, I dread to think what you might have me doing next. At some point, I have to be the adult. I can't let this keep escalating. It's sheer madness."

"But—"

"No buts." Marlee puts a hand over Cadence's mouth, silencing her. "It's way past your bedtime, and we've got lots to do tomorrow, so I want you up early."

She wriggles out from behind Cadence, then heaves her up off the sofa, holding hands with her all the way back to the bedroom. She'll have to get up extra early to go through all the rooms they fooled around in, making sure there's nothing suspicious or out of place.

A dropped earring. A lost button. A tube of lipstick. Bare footprints on the walls. All this worry just for a few kisses. Is it really worth it?

While Cadence is brushing her teeth in the bathroom, Marlee sits on the teen's bed, reflecting on that question, chewing over the day's activities. Before and after every kiss, she suffers a slight panic, reminding herself that it's wrong—so damn wrong. She feels it now, too, just waiting for Cadence to emerge, but she knows it won't last. She expects it to dissolve the instant their lips touch to kiss goodnight, but in reality, it dissolves as soon as Cadence steps out of the bathroom wearing that black lacy underwear.

"Oh, shit." She's totally unprepared for sexy Cadence. Where did the fuzzy guinea pig pajamas go?

Watching Cadence approach the bed, her heart thrums, loving and loathing how easily this young teen can disarm her, and she finds herself craving intimacy.

Intimacy she can't have.

In theory, she could always fall back into her casual arrangement with Rachel. But after the way Cadence reacted earlier, she dare not risk getting caught in bed with her again. Not only because she doesn't want to hurt Cadence, but because, well, even the mere thought of sharing intimacy with Rachel now somehow feels wrong. Like cheating.

Tired of being the voice of reason—or trying to be—and entranced by the beautiful young woman standing in front of her, she relinquishes all control as Cadence tilts her head up and kisses her, pushing her gently back onto the bed. It feels good to let go as Cadence—a girl who, under any other circumstance, would be perfectly free to be intimate with her in any and every way—straddles her thighs and leans over her for another kiss.

"You're so sexy, honey," Marlee manages to get out between lip-locks. "I want you so much."

As they kiss, she rubs Cadence's bare back, feeling the curve of her spine, her slender hips, and the rise of her buttocks. Without thinking, she slips her hands over Cadence's ass, enjoying how firm she is.

"Is it all right if I touch you like this?" she thinks to ask after the fact.

"Uh-huh." Cadence nods, thrilled and excited that Marlee wants to do more than just kiss her. "I like it."

They keep kissing, and Marlee can't resist edging her fingertips beneath the lace—she wants to feel bare ass. At that moment, Cadence does something remarkable: she starts to move. She starts to rock her hips back and forth, grinding herself against Marlee's pelvis.

Marlee moans into Cadence's mouth. Cadence is so inexperienced that she probably doesn't fully understand what she's doing, but Marlee certainly does: she's pleasuring herself. She's clamping down, rubbing her clit against Marlee's body. Will she make herself come? Has she ever had an orgasm? They've never spoken about it.

"Damn," Marlee mumbles quietly, finding the sensation of having young Cadence humping her more arousing than anything else she's ever experienced.

Cadence stops. "Is something wrong?"

"Oh, god, no!" Marlee slips her hands completely beneath the lace knickers, groping Cadence's bum, urging her to continue. "You surprise me in the best ways. You're wonderful."

"I want you to spend the whole night in my bed." Cadence grabs Marlee's hands, moving them from her rear to her lace covered breasts, trying to tempt her. "Will you? My parents aren't home."

"I wish I could, sweetheart." Marlee massages Cadence's chest. "You have no idea how much I want to, but I can't. Not tonight. Not now."

That's a lie. In all honesty, she very well could spend the whole night in Cadence's bed, were it not for one small, nagging problem: she needs to come. Her knickers are soaked through—she can feel it. She's been seeping with desire for most of the day—quite abundantly since lying on the games room sofa with Cadence—and she *needs* release.

She also needs Cadence to keep humping her, but that doesn't happen. Much to her disappointment— although she'd never let on—Cadence doesn't resume her gyrations. Instead, she rolls off and sprawls on the bed.

"Can we sleep together every night when we're on vacation?"

When Cadence says sleep, she really means sleep, but Marlee's body surges with uncontrollable arousal nonetheless.

"Maybe. We'll have to see how it goes." She remains outwardly calm.

This will be the first vacation they've ever taken alone.

Four days, three nights.

Alone.

Damn.

IT TAKES ABOUT THREE HOURS TO GET TO LYMINGTON IN the Ashlocks' chauffeur driven car, but they stop off at New Forest National Park in Hampshire on the way. Marlee says she fancies a picnic, but what she really fancies is Cadence. They eat sandwiches, indulge in some truffles that Marlee swiped from the cook's secret stash before they left Neverleigh, then make the chauffeur wait in the car while they take a slow stroll through the forest, hand in hand.

Whenever they find themselves in a secluded area—which they do often, entirely by design rather than luck—they lose themselves in kisses. Such tender kisses. Tender, grownup kisses with invading tongues and squeals of delight, followed by declarations of love and attraction.

This cherished time alone makes it exceedingly difficult for them both to get back in the car and revert to portraying their increasingly complicated relationship as being purely platonic. The façade of propriety is so easily shattered by an inadvertently loving gaze, an affectionate smile, or a wandering eye, followed by snickering and lower lip biting.

Her heart so full of love and passion, Marlee looks wistfully out of the window, watching the countryside roll by. Cadence's kisses are so, so perfect. Being intimate with her feels so natural, which is frightening and overwhelming, but extraordinarily exciting.

All she has to do is wait, she keeps telling herself. Kiss her, hold her, love her, and wait for her, her virginity the reward for their patience. But what about the Ashlocks and the debutante parties? Cadence could be wedded before they're ever in a position to act on their feelings, and the thought of having to stand by and watch her be married off against her will is becoming progressively more unbearable. She can only imagine what Cadence must be going through.

Mmm, Cadence.

It's not long into the second leg of the drive before she feels a warm hand brush against her knee and settle there. Should she move it away? She doesn't want to start a fuss over anything in front of the chauffeur. Sharing a restrained smile with Cadence, she opts to leave it there.

Cadence is growing bold, though. Not a minute later, she begins tugging on Marlee's skirt, pulling it up inch by inch until she gets the hem up over her knee.

Can the chauffeur see? Marlee glances up, checking his mirrors, wondering how far his line of sight extends. Probably not to their laps, she surmises. Still, why take any unnecessary risks? She angles her body toward Cadence and pats the space between them, inviting her to sit closer. It's not unusual for Cadence to be seen cuddling up to her nanny, and if they can tuck behind the driver's seat, there's a better chance they won't be caught touching inappropriately.

Reading her mind, Cadence shuffles closer and lets Marlee put an arm around her, drawing her into a hug, kissing the side of her head. When they're close, concealed behind the seat in front, Cadence puts her hand back on Marlee's knee.

Marlee can't help but notice that she's wearing the same t-shirt as yesterday: the one stretched tight across her chest. Those perky breasts are on display, and ... Marlee has to look twice to be certain. Cadence isn't wearing a bra! How had she not noticed that before? Her jacket must've been zipped up in the park.

Just knowing that her breasts are naked beneath the shirt has Marlee reaching a new level of fervor, consumed by an intense yearning to touch them again—and she can't wait. They're still twenty minutes away from Lymington, and she's desperate to cop a subtle feel. Under the guise of straightening Cadence's jacket, she grabs the lapel between her fingers and angles her thumb against one of Cadence's breasts, rubbing up and down. It might not be the most sophisticated act of fondling ever, but it's enough to elicit a response from the teen's nipple, which swells to a firm pebble in a matter of seconds.

Cadence snuggles tighter, starting to move her hand up Marlee's leg. As before, when she gets to the top of the stocking, Marlee prevents her from going any further. She reaches down and holds Cadence's hand, weaving their fingers together. Instead of pulling her away, though, she simply controls the direction of her exploration. Kneading Cadence's hand firmly up and down, she even goes so far as to uncross her legs and let Cadence's fingertips touch the bare skin of her inner thigh—albeit fleetingly.

This goes on for several minutes, and by the time they arrive at the Lymington bed and breakfast, neither one of them has much interest in exploring the picturesque seafront village.

Cadence's parents have reduced the booking to one family room containing a queen-size bed and a single, and it's delightfully quaint. The four-poster queen bed takes up most of it, with the little single pushed off to the side. At the far end, there's a dresser that doubles as a table for a kettle and a selection of complimentary teas and instant coffee, a little stack of cups beside them. Pictures of fishing boats and ornamental ship wheels adorn the walls—typical seaside décor. The en suite bathroom has a shower and soaker tub, almost every surface decorated with seashells and starfishes. All in all, it's cute.

Marlee opens the bedroom window, letting a warm gust of sea breeze into the room. Ahh, smells like childhood. It's comfortingly familiar, but so distant.

"I'm sorry your parents couldn't be here, darling." She takes in a lungful of salty air, reflecting on her own happy memories of a loving mother and father.

Cadence snorts, starting to unpack. "I'm not. This is perfect. It's so much better now they won't be anywhere near when we ... you know."

Marlee doesn't know. "When we what?"

"Have sex for the first time."

Those words rolls off her tongue far too nonchalantly for Marlee's liking.

"Have sex?" She could swear her heart just seized up. "Who said anything about us having sex? What makes you think we're ... ?"

"Oh." The smile drops from Cadence's lips, unable to hide her disappointment. "I thought you'd be ready. Aren't you ready?"

Marlee can't help it: she bursts out laughing at the ridiculousness of the question, and of their current predicament. Her sixteen-year-old would-be lover is asking *her* if she's ready for sex! Unfortunately, Cadence takes the spontaneous fit of laughter far too personally, and ends up locking herself in the bathroom for twenty minutes.

Apologetic, Marlee sits on the carpeted floor outside the en suite, trying to persuade her to come out. "I wasn't laughing at you, Cady."

"Yes, you were!" Muffled.

"No, I was laughing at the situation."

"What's so funny about me wanting to have sex with you?" Less muffled—she must've moved closer to the door.

Hearing Cadence say those words makes Marlee's heart flutter, her knickers dampening uncontrollably. Cadence really wants to have sex with her! That's so ... daunting, and she takes a moment to let it all sink in. Is this why Cadence doesn't date? Or ask about boys? Does she already have her heart set on her nanny?

"Think about it from my perspective," Marlee says at last. "My painfully young, virginal girlfriend just asked *me* if I was ready to put out. Shouldn't it be the other way around?"

Click.

The door unlocks, creaks open a little, and Cadence crawls out.

"Girlfriend?" she asks, hardly daring to hope that she heard Marlee correctly.

"Isn't that what you are?" Marlee gives up trying to pretend that this is anything other than an illicit love affair, especially since they've already committed so many indiscretions. "Isn't that what you want to be?"

"Does that mean we'll have sex?" Cadence crawls closer. "I don't care what the law says. I *am* old enough, and you do want to have me that way, don't you?"

How can Marlee possibly answer that? Admitting any of this out loud makes her feel like a degenerate sexual deviant. She can't bring herself to tell Cadence how she gets wet every time they kiss, or that last night she gave herself the most wonderful orgasm while fantasizing about the two of them being together. She just can't. All she can manage to say is:

"It's not as simple as that."

"Because you're afraid," Cadence very rightly guesses.

"Can you understand what this is like for me at all?" Marlee beckons her over, needing to have her near. "This isn't a harmless crush; it's a big deal."

"I know." Cadence breaks into a wide smile.

"Do you?" Marlee's brow is creased with a rarely seen tension. "Because I'm terrified that I might be falling very deeply in love with you, and I don't even know if you can—"

"I've been in love with you since I was thirteen." Cadence rests against her lap.

Marlee looks disbelieving. "I don't think thirteen-year-olds are capable of being in love, sweetheart. I'm not even sure sixteen-year-olds are. I know you love me—I'd never doubt that—but it's not the same as being *in* love with someone. The way I've begun to want you is very adult, and I don't understand how you can possibly have those feelings for me."

"Well, I do," Cadence says defiantly. "I dream about kissing you, sleeping with you, loving you, and that includes"—her cheeks flush endearingly—"giving you pleasure."

Marlee isn't immediately sure how to respond. She flounders briefly before managing to ask, "You dream about that? About making love with me?"

Cadence nods. "All the time."

"But ..." Marlee struggles to process that. "We've never even talked about ..."

Cadence rolls her eyes. "I know what sex is, Marlee. We have sex education in school. Just because my parents never wanted you to educate me, that doesn't mean I never *got* educated. Plus, there's television and the internet. I've even watched porn." She smiles proudly. "That's how I learned to kiss."

Marlee's jaw drops. "Porn?! I assumed you'd practiced on a boy!"

"Ewww." Cadence wrinkles her nose. "Why would I want to give up my first kiss to a horrid boy? I was saving it for you." Self-conscious about her lack of experience, she fidgets nervously with a frayed thread on the hem of her faded t-shirt. "I've been saving everything for you. I thought you'd like that."

Marlee's expression softens, her frown melting away. As her lips upturn, those shallow creases of happiness appear at the edges of her bright, glimmering eyes. Knowing now that their first kiss didn't just mark the commencement of their unlawful romance, but also that it was Cadence's first ever—her entrance into the adult world of intimacy—Marlee feels incredibly privileged. She doesn't want Cadence to think, even for a second, that she's being casual about receiving the gifts of her firsts.

"Oh, darling. I love knowing that I'm the only one." She instigates a kiss. "It makes everything we share even more special."

"You don't need to be afraid, Marlee," Cadence whispers, cuddling up to her. "I know what I want, and I know *who* I want. I always have." Another kiss. "That's why I waited." One more kiss. "I only want to be with you."

"Well, shall we start with dinner?" Marlee suggests, concerned that they might be about to get a tad sidetracked. "I think I owe you a date."

Yes, now it's definitely a date.

DINNER IS A QUIET AFFAIR, FULL OF INNUENDO AND CALF rubs. Cadence is wearing her debutante party dress, just as she said she would, and she looks delicious. Her hair's down, curled, her eyes painted with smoky eye shadow. She's even wearing some of Marlee's lipstick, and the shade looks good on her.

Also dressed to the nines, Marlee's out of her nanny outfit once again—it being banished to the suitcase for the duration of their trip, as per Cadence's strict orders. She's wearing a wine-colored dress, tight where it matters, with heels to accentuate her calves, and she feels like a sardine squished into a tin. The dress is fitted to her ribs so snugly she feels like there's a boa constrictor wrapped around her chest. She can barely breathe. Or is that because she's nervous?

Sex with Cadence! The more she wants it, the more she comes to realize that she's discovered a tenth circle of hell, reserved just for her: the nanny who abuses her position of trust by accepting the advances of her employers' daughter.

This is bad.

This is really, really bad.

There's something else on her mind, though, and in the end, she just comes right out and asks Cadence, "Are you gay?"

Indicative of the fact that she's been asking herself the same thing for quite some time, Cadence isn't at all caught off-guard by the question. She shrugs, not even looking up from her dinner plate. "I want you. Does that make me gay?"

Marlee doesn't want to put words in her mouth, so she leaves that question unanswered, turning her mind instead to a niggling concern that struck her when Cadence mentioned how old she was when her passions first surfaced.

"Did finding out that I was gay have any impact on ... your feelings?"

Marlee remembers a not-quite-fourteen-year-old Cadence coming to her innocently, a look of confusion plastered on her face, wanting to know what the word 'dyke' meant. That day, Marlee found out what Cadence's mother calls her behind her back, and Cadence found out that there's more to love than the union of a man and a woman.

Cadence nods, devouring the last bite of her dinner. "That's when I knew I wanted you for real. Before then, I didn't understand why I felt the way I did." She pushes her empty plate aside. "I didn't know two girls could do stuff that way."

Marlee suddenly makes a connection. "Is that when you started sneaking into my bed?"

Blushing, Cadence nods.

Now, Marlee has a suspicion. "Did you ever share a bed with your old nanny?"

Cadence shakes her head vigorously. "She was a wicked old bat. I just told you that so you wouldn't think I was being a freak." Still blushing, she shifts the focus of the conversation smoothly onto Marlee. "When did you start falling for me?"

"I'm not exactly sure." Marlee abandons the rest of her soup, still having difficulty believing that Cadence really wants what she thinks she wants. "I suppose it's been happening gradually, but still so much sooner than I would've liked. And I hope you don't think ... I mean, I want you to know that I don't ... with other girls your age. This isn't ... and I'm not ..."

I'm not a pervert. Why is that so difficult to say?

"It's okay, Marlee." Cadence reaches for her hand. "I'm not a little girl."

"I know." Marlee lets Cadence entwine their fingers. "But the law says I can't have you. Not yet."

"Well, the law is dumb," Cadence exclaims emphatically. "How does it make any sense at all that I can give myself to anyone but the one person I love? That's bollocks."

"The law's there to protect you, Cady." Marlee squeezes her hand reassuringly. "It's meant to prevent people in my position—often very much older people, like myself—from taking advantage of the hormone-fueled adolescents in their care."

"Very much older?" Cadence scoffs. "Do you know there's less age difference between us than there is between my mother and father? Nobody thinks their relationship is weird."

"Yes, but your father's exceptionally rich. He could marry a goat and people would still say things like: Gosh, I love your wife, she has really big eyes."

Cadence almost snorts her drink through her nose. Picturing what an awkward coupling that would be on the wedding night, her mind veers off in another direction. "Have you ever done it with a bloke?" She whispers that as if it's something dirty.

"Yes, that's how I found out I was gay."

That makes Cadence giggle. "Was it yucky? I've seen straight porn. It looks yucky."

"Men are hairy and smelly, and testicles are ugly. Give me a pair of nice, smooth legs, a handful of boobs, and a wet, velvety vagina any day."

Cadence fidgets with nervous excitement, thrilled by this new sexual openness. "Have you been with lots of women?"

Marlee shakes her head. "I haven't really had the opportunity."

"Because of your job?" Cadence looks unnecessarily apologetic.

Nodding, Marlee smiles warmly. "A very worthwhile sacrifice." She pauses and lowers her voice. "But I am exceptionally good in bed if that's what you're worried about." Wink.

Cadence's cheeks burn. "Are you saying we're going to have sex tonight?"

She says that a little too loudly, and Marlee flits her eyes around the restaurant quickly, making sure no-one's paying any attention. They're not.

"I'm saying"—she leans close, whispering—"I won't deny you anything that feels natural and easy between us. Is that fair?"

Cadence plays with Marlee's feet under the table, grinning. "Do you want pudding?"

"Absolutely." Marlee smirks, asking the waiter for the bill.

She's in a heightened state of arousal on the walk back to the bed and breakfast, Cadence's arm looped through hers. She's so certain Cadence will initiate intimacy tonight that she's momentarily taken aback when—dressed in enticing black silk lingerie—she steps out from the en suite bathroom and finds Cadence already in bed.

Curled on her side, she's sound asleep in the queen bed, her chestnut hair splayed across the pillow. Most telling of all, she's wearing those fuzzy guinea pig pajamas again, and Marlee knows what all of this adds up to: she's changed her mind.

Climbing into bed with her, Marlee smiles, kisses the side of her head, whispers goodnight, and retreats into her own space. Truth be told, she's somewhat relieved. Everything is perfect just the way it is, except that the build-up to this rather anti-climactic moment has left her with a persistent heat between her legs.

Dare she tend to herself? If she's quiet, and Cadence is asleep, why not? She needs to come again. She *wants* to come again. Slipping a hand between her legs, she tiptoes her fingers over a wet patch in the gusset of her knickers. This'll be quick.

Careful not to jar the bed, she worms a hand inside her undies and begins touching herself. Nothing vigorous, just a gentle tickle over and around her clit. God, that feels good. She spreads her legs and holds her breath, hoping to bring herself to peak in under a minute.

She's close.

So close.

Until ...

"What're you doing?" Cadence rolls over.

Marlee freezes, too afraid to move a muscle. "I'm sorry, darling. Did I wake you?"

"Are you flicking your bean?" Cadence peeks under the duvet.

Marlee takes a long time to answer, distracted by the unfamiliar phrasing. "Yes."

"Why did you stop?"

"I thought you were sleeping." Marlee starts to pull her hand back from her clit. "If I knew—"

Cadence stops her, urging her hand back inside her knickers. "Keep doing it."

"Cady ..." Marlee gasps as her fingers reconnect with her needy flesh.

"I want to watch."

Marlee groans. Really? Cadence wants to watch her come? Damn. In no position to argue—her body on the brink of climax already—she starts 'flicking her bean' again, maintaining eye contact with Cadence right up until the crest of her orgasm comes crashing down over her.

Biting hard on her lower lip, she tilts her head back, her eyes closed, her legs jerking and twitching as she whimpers sensually, her cunt pulsing.

"Wow." Cadence puts her hand on Marlee's thigh, feeling the tremors, completely fascinated by them. "What just happened?" Porn hasn't prepared her for this.

"I had a really strong orgasm," Marlee whispers breathlessly. "Have you never had one?"

Cadence seems uncertain. "I don't think so."

Marlee rolls to look at her. "You've never pleasured yourself?"

Slightly red in the cheeks, the innocent girl shakes her head.

"Well, I think you nearly came last night, when you were rubbing yourself on me." Marlee forms an idea. "Do you remember how that felt?"

Cadence nods, now blushing fiercely. "Hot."

"Would you like to try again?"

Cadence doesn't object, so Marlee pulls her closer, lifting one of her legs up.

"Here"—she pulls Cadence's leg over her hip—"tell me how this feels."

Angling her thigh against Cadence's core, she holds the teen's bum tightly and thrusts forward, generating delightful friction against her crotch.

Cadence closes her eyes. "It feels ..."

Suddenly, Marlee's thigh rubs against her clit and her body jolts.

"Oh! Nice."

Marlee keeps gently humping her until she starts to spasm.

"Marlee ..." Cadence whispers, clutching at her shoulder. "Oh, Marlee!"

Cadence's orgasm is incredible, her virgin body quivering in Marlee's arms. When it passes, she flops onto her back, sighing contentedly.

"*That's* an orgasm?! I've felt that before!" she recalls with glee. "I woke up as I was having it. My ... umm ... my place was throbbing and squeezing, and I thought I had to pee, but then it passed so I just tucked myself against you and—"

"Me?" Marlee can't help interjecting.

"Uh-huh." Cadence nods, not understanding the importance of the fact. "We were sleeping together."

Marlee's heart almost bursts. Cadence had a wet dream! While they were lying together, she'd had her first orgasm and neither of them had known about it.

Marlee tingles with excitement. "Good god."

"What?"

"You were lying next to me, all hot and horny, and I had no idea." Marlee turns onto her back, pulling Cadence to her chest. "I bet your knickers were so fucking damp."

Cadence giggles. "I like hearing you talk like this."

"What? Dirty?"

"No. Well, yes. Just not holding anything back. I like that."

"Me, too." Marlee kisses her head. "I hadn't realized how much tension there was between us until suddenly I could kiss you and hold you, and love you the way I've wanted to love you for so many months. I don't think I've ever been this happy."

That's true. Sex or no sex, that's true.

Chapter Thirteen

MARLEE PRESSES HER CHEEK AGAINST THE COOL PILLOW, feeling sunlight on her face and salty air in her lungs. This is the first morning in a long time that she hasn't woken up to any particular schedule, and just to lie quietly, basking in the ecstasy of spending a guilt-free night in bed with Cadence, is pure bliss. She didn't even need sex last night. It felt perfect just the way they were.

Kissing.

Holding.

So much kissing.

Cadence comes out of the bathroom, wearing nothing more than her t-shirt and knickers, rubbing her hair dry with a towel. "You're awake!" She leaps onto the bed.

Without giving Marlee a chance to say anything back, she dives on top of her, bombarding her with kisses. All Marlee can do is whine her approval.

Cadence is being so passionate and so forceful. What the hell's gotten into her this morning? Where's the bashful girl in guinea pig pajamas she just shared a bed with? Who cares? Marlee slips her hands inside a pair of cotton knickers, groping Cadence's ass.

"Mmm, good morning." She stretches beneath her. "What a nice way to wake up."

"I like this, Marlee." Cadence plants one more kiss on her, then wriggles into bed beside her. "And I'm sorry about last night. It won't happen again."

"Whatever are you talking about, sweetheart?" Marlee fingers a lock of damp chestnut hair. "Last night was wonderful."

"No, it wasn't," Cadence mumbles forlornly. "I panicked."

"I know," Marlee says, understanding. No explanation needed.

"I wasn't really sleeping when you came to bed." Cadence feels she ought to confess. "I just had so many butterflies, and—"

"Sshhh." Marlee kisses her. "No apologies."

"But—"

Another kiss. "Don't, Cady."

"Don't what?"

"Don't try to make yourself do things because you think it's what I want." Marlee brings her young lover closer. "I'll wait for you."

"Huh?"

"Till you're ready. If you're worried about Rachel, you needn't be. I won't touch her, or anyone else. There are plenty of ways you and I can be intimate without going all the way, and loving you properly is so much more important than my own selfish need for sex."

Marlee expects the promise of fidelity to cheer Cadence, alleviating whatever burden she was placing on herself. Instead, it seems to make her even more dejected.

"If we wait too long, I'll be engaged." She sinks into the bed, staring up at the ceiling. "My mother's hoping to have me promised to someone at seventeen, and married at eighteen." She rolls onto her side, away from Marlee. "And you be won't be my nanny anymore." Her voice cracks. "You'll be gone. So if we wait, there'll be nothing to wait *for*."

She's right: their time together is finite, and slipping away from them by the day.

"Darling, try not to fret so much about the future." Marlee snuggles up behind her. "Who knows what it'll bring?" She squeezes Cadence's shoulder, turning her into an embrace. "And let's not let such dark thoughts mar this weekend together." She gives her a brief peck on the lips, trying to lighten the mood. "What do you want to do today? Any ideas?"

Her face lighting up again, Cadence lunges for the bedside table and retrieves a map. Opening it, she finds Lymington, then trails her finger west, jabbing at a particular spot.

"I thought we could go here."

She's pointing to Milford-on-Sea, another seaside village. It's only ten minutes away by car.

Marlee peers over her shoulder, recognizing the place immediately. "That's ..." She glances at Cadence, wondering if she has any idea of its significance.

She does.

"That's your village, isn't it?" She smiles. "That's where you're from?"

Marlee nods, on the verge of tears. "Is that why you picked this place?"

"Uh-huh." Cadence's smile grows. "I wanted to surprise you."

It worked.

"How did you know?" Marlee daren't blink for fear of setting her tears free.

"I snuck into my father's study and peeped at your employment file. He keeps files on all the staff. He's such a creeper."

Endorphins surging, Marlee wants to show her appreciation for the effort. "Do you trust me, Cady?"

"Of course I trust you. Wh—"

Marlee grabs her, throws her down on the bed, moves her legs apart, and wiggles her way between them. Lying over Cadence, she fondles one breast over her t-shirt while kissing her. The kisses start on her lips, trail down her neck—almost to her chest—then work back up to her lips.

Suddenly breaking the kisses off, Marlee kneels between Cadence's legs and thrusts her pelvis forward, grinding their sexes together.

Cadence yelps excitedly. "Holy crap, Marlee!"

"I love you, Cadence." Marlee bends to kiss her again, continuing to hump her tenderly. "I can give you so much pleasure without ever laying a finger on you. Now lift up your legs."

Cadence does as Marlee asks, the act of raising her legs to Marlee's waist serving to tilt her pelvis up, allowing Marlee to directly stimulate her clit with every thrust. It's sensual, erotic, and with only two thin layers of cotton between them, it feels almost bare.

"Oh!" Cadence wraps her arms around Marlee's neck. "Yes!"

At first, she thinks this is entirely for her own enjoyment, but it soon becomes apparent that Marlee—her breathing quickened, mewling soft noises of ecstasy—is getting just as much satisfaction from it.

"I really do love you, Cady." She clutches at Cadence's ass, keeping the teen's hips angled upward. "So much it hurts."

In only a few minutes, Cadence feels her orgasm building, the heat between her legs seeming to encompass her entire abdomen, her body on fire beneath Marlee. She begins to pant, her eyes wide as the now familiar sensation of sexual climax starts to rise in her.

"Marlee! I'm—" She cries out, her orgasm overtaking her.

Grinding more firmly, Marlee gyrates directly on Cadence's clit as her own climax hits. "Oh, god!" Her legs are trembling so much she almost collapses.

She holds herself tight against Cadence until her peak starts to wane, breathing heavily, their bodies a bundle of shivers.

"Was that okay?" she asks then, gazing fondly at her lover.

"What did we just do?" Cadence is breathless, her face flushed, her nipples hard beneath her too-tight t-shirt. "It was epic."

"It was the same thing we did last night, but for both of us this time." Marlee maneuvers out from between her legs, dropping down next to her. "Did you enjoy it?"

"Is it sex?"

"It's a kind of sex we can have without you giving anything up. You understand?"

Cadence nods. "It was amazing. I felt you come against me." She looks down at her crotch. "I think you made my knickers damp."

Marlee laughs. "Probably. Mine are soaked."

"Can I peek?"

Marlee parts her legs and lets Cadence look up her negligee, but her knickers are black and it's difficult to see clearly. Cadence extends a hand toward her, seeking a quick feel, but hesitates halfway.

"Do you mind?"

"Darling, from now on, you can always touch me. You don't have to ask."

Cadence moves her hand up to the gusset of Marlee's knickers, rubbing her index and middle fingers over the saturated fabric, feeling the cleft of Marlee's vagina beneath, making her murmur.

"Wow." Cadence withdraws. "Do you always get so wet?"

"Lately, yes. You turn me on a lot." Marlee rolls onto her side, propping herself up on her elbow. "Are you really taking me to see my family?"

Cadence snuggles up to her. "I want to give you something special. My parents never ask you what you want. You never get anything."

"But I already have the best thing in the world."

Cadence is genuinely clueless.

"You, you daft apeth." Marlee kisses her, sucking on her baby pink lips. "As long as I have you, nothing else matters."

That's a lovely sentiment, but Cadence isn't convinced by it.

"Everyone should get to spend time with their family, Marlee." She flings an arm around her waist. "How long's it been since you last visited home?"

Tears invade Marlee's eyes again, but she refuses to set them free. "Almost three years."

"Are you serious?!"

Cadence isn't sure what she was expecting to hear, but it wasn't that. She doesn't recollect Marlee ever being away from her for any length of time, but she always assumed that visits, while perhaps rare, must be occurring somehow.

Marlee tucks a lock of drying hair behind Cadence's ear, gazing affectionately at her. "I don't get time off from taking care of you, honey."

"But—"

Marlee stops her. "I don't *want* time off from taking care of you. I love taking care of you, and I knew what I was giving up when I accepted the position as your nanny."

"But your family ..."

"I meet my sister for lunch a few times a year, when she's not off gallivanting around the country with her eccentric hippie boyfriend. My parents come up the odd time, too. It's always very brief, but we've grown accustomed to it. Ultimately, I'm paid a fair wage, my family's income is supplemented by your family's kind donations, and I get to spend every minute with you. It's a fine arrangement."

Fine, but definitely not fair. Other nannies get annual vacation time to spend at home with their families, but the Ashlocks made it very clear from the outset that they wouldn't be able to accommodate her taking any time for herself. In lieu of that, they offered to provide her family additional financial support—an offer she simply couldn't decline.

It did all work out for the best, though.

The spectacular orgasm she just experienced is a testament to that.

MARLEE PAYS FOR THE TEN MINUTE TAXI FARE ON HER personal credit card, so that their little excursion to Milford-on-Sea might remain concealed from the Ashlocks. They'd never approve of Cadence meeting her family, which is precisely why none of her relatives have ever been invited to spend time at Neverleigh, and why visits have to be conducted only when Cadence is occupied elsewhere.

The reason? Because the Meeks family are working class folk, and Cadence has been instructed not to mingle outside of her own social group. Such interaction might detrimentally blur the dividing line between their two very different worlds. Heaven forbid.

In fact, Cadence has been so shut off from the realities of life that Marlee wonders how she'll react to the tiny former council house they're about to visit. Will it seem strange to her that an entire family can live in a box not much bigger than Neverleigh's grand entrance hallway? Will she laugh and offend someone accidentally? Will she feel uncomfortable? Cadence is used to space—emotionally and physically—and that's not something you'll ever find in the Meeks household, where everyone is always rubbing shoulders.

Nervous, Marlee stands on the curb in front of a red brick house at the end of a quiet cul-de-sac, holding Cadence's hand. The front garden is well-tended, the flower beds weeded, the grass kept short, and the front door has a fresh coat of white paint. Somewhere nearby, children are playing. Seagulls are squawking, fighting over the day-old, discarded leftovers of someone's fish and chips. The smell of fish pervades, someone in the cul-de-sac having recently gutted a fresh catch.

She looks down at her clothes, wondering if she picked the right outfit: deliberately faded jeans; white, low cut camisole; a loose cotton shirt, buttoned halfway. She wanted to look nice, but not fancy. Why had she put on such expensive shoes? She wiggles her toes inside a pair of black, patent leather stilettos—the same ones she wore last night.

Shoes are her one weakness. She likes the way a nice pair of high heels makes her feel—feminine and sexy—and she likes the way Cadence admires them on her. Cadence herself doesn't own any, and once sprained her ankle while trying to walk in a pair she pilfered from Marlee's room.

Today, as most days, she's wearing canvas athletics, raggedy jeans, and a motif t-shirt that proclaims her undying devotion to some band Marlee's never heard of. She hides her family's money well. She didn't even brush her hair this morning after she washed it, she just scrunched it up into a messy ponytail. She looks beautiful. Carelessly and effortlessly beautiful.

Taking a deep breath, Marlee leads them down the garden path—literally—and rings the doorbell. As she does, Cadence gives her hand a comforting squeeze. Is her anxiety really that apparent? How silly, she thinks. This is her home, not Buckingham Palace!

She steals a peck on the lips. "I love you."

The kiss is thrilling. Not because it's erotic, or passionate in any way, but simply because it's outdoors. Someone could see! For the briefest of moments, Marlee feels as though she's in a normal relationship.

When the door opens, it's a small boy who answers. He appears to be about six years old, wearing baggy thrift store shorts that he'll probably grow into a year from now, and a plain t-shirt that's covered in dirt and grass stains. With hazel eyes and a thick mop of blonde hair, he definitely looks like a Meeks, but rather embarrassingly, Marlee doesn't immediately recognize him. He could be her nephew, or he could be some random neighborhood boy who's being paid to help her father do some work in the garden.

"Edward?" she asks tentatively.

The young boy cocks his head, narrows his eyes, and scrutinizes her for a few moments, wondering how he knows this stranger. Then, a lightning bolt strikes.

"Auntie Lee!"

Forgetting to invite them inside, he darts back into the house, squealing excitedly and calling for his mother. "Mumma! Mumma! Auntie Lee's come home!"

Grinning, Marlee steps indoors, pulling a reluctant Cadence with her.

"Come on, my girl." She tugs her young lover's arm. "It's all right."

She has to coax Cadence into the hallway like an unwilling horse, knowing that, for her, this is where the culture shock begins. In her world, no-one would ever just walk into another's house—even family. You'd have to wait to be greeted on the doorstep, and then be formally invited inside. The distinct lack of ceremony is undoubtedly disconcerting.

Once in, the entrance hallway presents the next learning curve. It's small and narrow, with an overfilled coat rack on the wall and a disorganized pile of shoes on the floor. Marlee kicks off her high heels and discards them on the pile, encouraging Cadence to do the same.

"It's polite to do so," she explains, Cadence being unaware of the custom.

As they make their way into the living room, the young boy drags a blonde-haired woman in from the back garden, insisting that Auntie Lee is at the door.

"Don't be ridiculous, Eddie," the woman grumbles. "You know full well that Aunt Marlee can't leave—" She cuts herself off when she looks up and sees Marlee standing in the living room. "Oh, my good gracious!"

"I told ya!" Eddie sticks his tongue out at her.

The woman clips his ear lightly. "Enough of your lip. Go fetch your grammy and grampa." She sends him away, then dashes at Marlee with a bear hug. "Sissy!"

Marlee drops Cadence's hand to hug her sister back, and Cadence blends into the background, more than happy to stand aside and watch this reunion unfold before her.

There's a clear family resemblance. The woman, while a handful of years younger than Marlee, has the same face shape and the same eyes. Her hair's a lighter shade, but she has Marlee's lips and cheek bones. In a short, halter neck dress, it's quite apparent that she also has Marlee's figure.

A few seconds later, a heavy-set, gray-haired man in trousers, suspenders, a wife-beater t-shirt, and a tweed flat cap enters the room. He's covered with dirt, sweat coating his brow, and as his pale, weak eyes fall upon Marlee, he beams a smile that reveals two missing teeth.

"Well, I bloody never!" He takes the flat cap off his head, wipes his brow with it, then puts it back in place.

He's followed by his wife, Marlee's mother, who's second in line to give Marlee a warm welcome.

"Oh, my dearest." She pulls Marlee into her skinny arms. "I didn't expect to see you back here for another twelve months or thereabouts."

Twelve months from now, if the Ashlocks have their way, Cadence will be engaged.

Twelve months from now, Marlee will almost certainly be unemployed.

The reminder hurts.

Marlee's mother is gray-haired and frail. She looks like a twig draped in fabric, her homemade, ankle-length dress faded from so many washes. She peers at the slight young girl standing sheepishly behind her eldest daughter.

"Who's your friend, dear?"

"Oh! I'm sorry. How rude!" Smiling so much her face hurts, Marlee takes Cadence by the hand and pulls her to the center of the room. "This gorgeous young thing is Cadence. Cadence Ashlock."

In a heartbeat, the atmosphere in the room changes. Smiles drop, replaced by shock. Every Meeks in the room—including the little one—stands up straight, and they show respect by dipping their heads slightly, all eye contact lost.

Mister Meeks swipes the cap off his head. "It's an honor to meet you, Miss."

Marlee's mother is immediately flustered, and attempts to perform a little curtsey without really knowing how to go about it. "An Ashlock in my little house? Well, I never!" She almost trips on her own ankles and grabs hold of a chair back for support.

The display of deference makes Cadence feel decidedly awkward.

"Oh ... umm ..." At a loss, she looks up at Marlee for help. "Make them stop."

"There's no need for all this nonsense. Really truly," Marlee assures them. "You don't need to stand on ceremony with Cady. She's an Ashlock in name only, and you should treat her no different from me."

Marlee's sister recovers herself first.

"I'm Isla." She holds her hand out. "Marlee's little sister."

Cadence thinks they're going to shake hands, but once Isla has a hold, she doesn't let go.

"This is my son, Edward." She points to the little boy, starting to lead Cadence toward the back garden. "Now I really hope you like lemonade. I just made a fresh batch."

After several hours of much needed catching up, with Cadence happily spilling fond memories of the last two and a half years spent with Marlee, giving the Meeks family a hitherto unseen glimpse into the very private relationship they've shared during this time, conversation starts to flow easily from one topic to another.

They discuss Mister Meeks' work in the garden, which has him covered in dirt, and Cadence learns how to grow potatoes. Then, she's quizzed by Isla on what it's like to attend a posh private school, and whether or not the boys are any hotter there than at state school. In answer, Cadence says that she's not really interested in boys, then flashes Marlee a coy smile. If anyone suspects anything, they don't say.

Later, while Cadence kicks a ball around the garden with Eddie, Marlee and Isla sit together on a swing seat, rocking idly back and forth, chatting over more glasses of lemonade. Every now and again, Cadence glances over at Marlee, just to share a smile.

"How old is she now?" Isla enquires.

"She just turned sixteen." Marlee doesn't take her eyes off Cadence.

Having played lacrosse for years, Cadence is fit and agile, her body used to physical exertion and sport. She's energetic, with bucket loads of stamina, barely breaking a sweat despite the rising summer sun.

"And how long have you been in love with her?" Isla asks next.

Marlee feels her heart plummet to the pit of her stomach. How does Isla know? What had she done to give it away? Had she said the wrong thing? Or touched Cadence in the wrong way? This is something she's been fearing in the back of her mind: growing too comfortable with the inappropriate closeness between them and slipping up in front of others. Has it happened already? In only a few days.

Isla snickers at her sister's panicked expression. "I know what you look like when you're in love, Marl. You can't hide anything in those eyes of yours."

"I know it's wrong." Marlee breaks her gaze away from Cadence. "I've tried not to feel this way, but she makes me so happy."

"Are you sleeping with her?"

Horrified, her eyes wide, Marlee glares at her sister. "No! Absolutely not!"

"All right, all right." Isla holds up a pacifying hand. "I was only asking. No need to bite my sodding head off."

"Well, shit, Isla. What a question!"

"Touchy subject obviously." Isla takes a sip of her lemonade, remarkably unfazed by the fact that her older sister is in love with a sixteen-year-old. "Do you *want* to shag her?"

"Isla!" Marlee's cheeks flare red. "It's against the law! I'm her nanny!"

Still calm, Isla shrugs. "Well, the law don't take into account the fact that her lot marry so bloody young. If you dither about too much, you'll lose her to somebody else, won't you?"

Marlee sighs, wishing it were as straightforward as Isla's making it out to be. Even if Cadence's age wasn't an issue, she'd still have Mister and Missus Ashlock to contend with. They want their daughter to marry someone wealthy, and without the wage she earns working for them, she doesn't have two pennies to rub together. No-one in the Ashlocks' social circle marries for love. Ever. Besides which, the point is moot: Cadence isn't even ready to be deflorated. She wants to be, but she's not, so this little discussion changes nothing.

"I'll lose her anyway." Marlee sips from her glass. "But she gave a relatively poor performance at her first debutante party. I highly doubt her behavior will have attracted any interest, so that might buy us some more time."

"And is that all you want?" Isla sets her drink aside. "More time?"

Marlee fails to answer, suddenly realizing that forever wouldn't even be long enough.

It's a soul destroying thought.

She finishes her lemonade in silence and balances her glass on her knee, massaging her brow. "What can I do, Isla?"

"I can't answer that for you, darl', but I reckon you should stop punishing yourself for the way you feel at any rate. Can't nobody help that." Isla takes Marlee's empty lemonade glass and gets up, beckoning Eddie over. "Come on, you little scruff bag. Let's get lunch on."

While Eddie follows Isla indoors, Cadence drops down on the swing seat beside Marlee. She barely has a chance to take a breath before Marlee pounces on her, pressing a deep, needy kiss on her dehydrated lips, invading her mouth with unrestrained passion.

In desperate need of oxygen, Cadence peels herself away. "Whoa, Marlee!" She smiles nervously, looking around, wondering what could've gotten Marlee so hungry for a kiss that she's willing to risk getting caught. "Aren't you worried someone will see?"

The swing seat canopy has them fairly well concealed, but Marlee's too emotional to care anyway. She rests her forehead on Cadence's shoulder, nuzzling her neck.

"I don't want to lose you."

Cadence never gets to ask what that means. Eddie returns and summons them to the kitchen, whereupon Cadence is taught how to pod peas while Marlee laughs, teases, and flirts lightly. Lunch is consumed, and an invitation to dinner is accepted, promptly followed by an invitation to spend the night. Of course, that means sharing a bed.

Marlee's old room is now Eddie's, so Isla offers up her bedroom to them for the night, happy to bundle with her son, even though he seems somewhat put out at the prospect of having to share a bed with his mother.

Concerned that Cadence, unaccustomed as she is to the concept of bundling, and needing to have the term explained to her, might be uncomfortable with such an arrangement, Marlee's father asks if they mind sleeping together.

To that, Isla laughs knowingly. "I'm sure they'll cope just fine."

And they do.

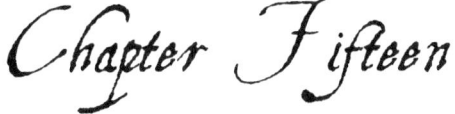

WEARING SKIMPY COTTON NIGHTDRESSES BORROWED from Isla, Marlee and Cadence clamber into bed, Cadence pausing on the way to admire herself in a mirror, declaring excitedly that she'd very much like to start wearing lingerie like this to bed every night.

The declaration receives no complaints from Marlee, who's been poring keenly over Cadence's sleek, cotton-clad form since she first put it on, admiring the way it clings to her hips and shows off that astoundingly curvaceous posterior. Though she'd never have considered spanking Cadence as a punishment, she's damn well thinking about doing it now. Just a gentle slap against a bare buttock, leaving a pink handprint behind.

Would Cadence like that? Would it turn her on? Should she ask? No, not yet, she tells herself, pushing the thought to the very back of her mind. It's too soon. Anyway, despite Isla's encouragement, she wants to keep her promise to Cadence. She said she'd wait, and she will. She'll kiss and caress, rubbing and thrusting against her for their mutual pleasure, but she'll wait patiently for more, buying herself time to think of a solution to their predicament.

The latter thought must be showing in her expression, she realizes, as Cadence shuffles across the bed, her brow slightly creased.

"Are you happy?" she asks, edging closer.

Marlee forces the encroaching look of worry from her face. "I'm not sure I've ever been happier." She reaches forward and sweeps Cadence's bangs out of her eyes. "You have no idea what this visit means to me. Thank you so much."

She holds her arms open, inviting Cadence against her for kisses, and once the mutually hungered for lip-locks begin, they don't stop for several minutes. Marlee slips her hand under Cadence's nightdress, seeking out her bum, thinking nothing of navigating inside her knickers to touch bare skin. Once her hand's inside, she squeezes and kneads, digging her nails into Cadence's flesh, and it's not long before she starts to get a little carried away.

As the kissing intensifies, her hand wanders to Cadence's hip, clutching at a delightfully prominent hip bone, sliding from hip to thigh and back again. The up and down movement tugs Cadence's knickers lower, the fabric stretched to accommodate her hand inside.

"Marlee ..." Cadence whispers against her lips.

Thinking she's overstepped—her hand just inches away from Cadence's most precious area—Marlee retreats to the safe zone: buttocks. But that's not the reason Cadence whispered her name.

"My body tingles when I'm close to you like this," she says softly, her own adventurous hand exploring the gloriously sensual, womanly shape of Marlee's waist and hip. "It tingles and aches in different places."

Marlee can figure out well enough where it tingles—her body's reacting just the same—but she has to ask, "Where do you ache, darling?"

Cadence sits up, reaching for the hem of her borrowed nightdress. "Can I show you?"

Marlee nods, at a loss for words. Is this really happening? Is Cadence really going to undress in front of her? This time yesterday, she was wearing guinea pig pajamas and pretending to be asleep. Now, she's stripping practically naked!

"They're wonderful, darling," Marlee reassures her, pinching a delightful nipple between her fingers, desperately aware that she's salivating. "May I kiss them?"

"Uh-huh." Cadence nods, her lower lip caught between her teeth. "I want you to kiss me everywhere."

Fighting the urge to tear off Cadence's knickers and press her lips elsewhere, Marlee brings her mouth to one of Cadence's breasts, still fondling the other. She bumps her bottom lip against the nipple, letting her warm breath tease it before sucking it into her mouth.

The stiff bud is so dainty, swelling as she closes her lips around the whole areola, and Cadence whimpers as she nips it with her teeth, pulling on it ever so gently, dragging her teeth along it. She could spend the whole night like this, just kissing, licking, sucking, pinching, biting, pulling—so much kissing.

But Cadence wants more.

"Can I see yours?" She tries to sneak a peek down Marlee's nightdress. "Can I touch them?"

Marlee's nipples become rigid at the mere suggestion of Cadence's touch, and she sits up, pulling her nightdress off over her head. Even the simple act of exposing herself feels deeply erotic, knowing that this is the first time Cadence has ever seen another woman's naked breasts. Porn doesn't count; this is the real thing. It's Cadence's first look, first touch, and first lick, and it's happening with her! How divine!

Ample breasts revealed, Marlee lies on her back, honey blonde hair flowing over her chest and the pillow. Rolling over for a closer look, Cadence moves locks of hair aside, clearing the view, her eyes wide with wonder.

"Jeepers, Marlee." She scoops one D-cup boob into her hand. "They're so big."

Her touch is exquisite. She's slow, gentle, and exploratory, taking her time to learn the intricacies of Marlee's body, absorbing every detail.

She swirls her finger around the areola, making it puff up, then she brushes her palm against the nipple, feeling its erectness. Finally, she bends forward and runs her tongue over it, licking it before drawing it into her hot mouth.

Much to Marlee's surprise, she feels an orgasm building.

"Oh, shit." She fists Cadence's hair the same way she would if she were receiving oral sex. "That feels incredible."

She places Cadence's hand on her other breast, encouraging her to knead it, pressing firmly. Both breasts are tingling, her cunt throbbing, weeping, and pulsing, erotic sensations coursing through her body.

Cadence is sucking and licking on one swollen nipple, massaging it with her tongue, using her mouth as if she's performing cunnilingus. Is she practicing? Is this a test run? Her face is pressed against Marlee's chest, her tongue and lips working her bedmate to climax.

Marlee's imagination starts to run rampant. What would this feel like between her legs?

That thought sends her over the edge.

"Christ, Cady." Shivers erupt in her body.

When she's still again, Cadence lifts up her head. "Did you just come?"

Marlee nods. "You get me so worked up."

"Do you always come like that?"

"Never before." Marlee closes her eyes, relishing the echoes of her peak.

Unwilling to let her get too relaxed in case she prematurely nods off, Cadence bumps noses with her. "Marlee?"

"Yes, darling?"

"I'm ... I need ..." She doesn't know how to ask for it. "I can feel my heartbeat in my ... umm ... my down there place."

"Your cunt?" Marlee peers at her though half-closed eyes. "Go on," she urges, smirking. "I want to hear you say it."

A blush of shyness blooms on Cadence's cheeks. "I can't."

"Why not? If you're going to do adult things, you should use adult words."

"Don't make fun of me, Marlee." Cadence pulls Marlee onto her side, their breasts pressing together. "I think I'm really wet, and I need you to touch me."

Marlee loses the smirk. Did Cadence really just say that? Did she just ask for sex? Holy fuck. All other thoughts evaporate, and suddenly, Marlee's entire being is consumed with the thought of making love to her paramour.

Without waiting for her to make a move, Cadence takes Marlee's hand and pulls it down under the duvet. "Make me come, Marlee."

She parts her legs, forcing Marlee's hand inside her knickers.

"Cady," Marlee whispers, her fingertips edging into a thick mound of wiry pubic hair, hesitating to go further. "Honey, are you sure you're ready for this?"

"I want you to touch me the way you touched yourself last night."

Marlee has no idea whether or not she should stop this from happening, but she puts the concern out of her mind. She *wants* to give Cadence pleasure. Working her fingers down through the full bloom of untamed curls, she finds the nub of Cadence's clit and the top of her cleft.

"Oh, my god." Her insides spasm as she touches her young lover for the first time.

Cadence is so wet, her skin slick and hot. Losing herself in this perfect moment, Marlee rolls Cadence onto her back, cradling her neck, kissing her as she tickles her clit. Needing more, she runs her middle finger down between Cadence's labia, using her fore and ring fingers to add extra sensation.

When Cadence instinctively spreads her legs wider, Marlee can't resist pushing one fingertip deeper, probing her tight opening, teasing her with the offer of penetration.

"Do you like that, darling?"

"Mm-hmm." Cadence nods, wiggling her hips up, encouraging Marlee inside. "Feels really good."

Spurred on by her receptiveness, Marlee pushes in all the way, moving her finger in fast circles, feeling how wonderfully tight she is.

Both of them moan. Cadence moans because she's overcome with sensation, and Marlee moans because she's inside Cadence. Inside hot, wet, unbelievably tight Cadence.

"You feel amazing," Marlee whispers, close to reaching another orgasm of her own.

She keeps probing and stroking, her palm rubbing against Cadence's clit. In just a few short minutes, she has Cadence clutching at the bed sheets.

"Oh, Marlee ..." She's trying to be quiet, fully conscious of the fact that this house is small, and the walls are paper thin.

"I love hearing you say my name when you're about to come," Marlee eggs her on.

Done deal.

Cadence lets herself go. "I'm coming, Marlee!"

THE NEXT DAY PASSES LIKE A WHIRLWIND: MUCH TOO fast. Marlee and Cadence stay at Milford-on-Sea for breakfast, lunch, and dinner, but decline the offer to spend another night. While they cite reasons such as a change of clothes and a very early start in the morning, the truth is, this'll be their last night away from Neverleigh, and they want to spend it alone.

Giddy with excitement, they tumble into their bedroom in the bed and breakfast, kissing and groping with a fervor that began in the taxi on their way here. They'd kissed and cuddled far too much, Marlee relying on the hope that the driver wouldn't think anything of the obvious age difference, and Cadence too horny to care what he thought anyway.

As soon as they're safely confined to their room, Cadence instructs Marlee to sit on the bed while she lets down her hair and strips, her lacy knickers being the last thing to hit the floor.

"Goddamn, Cady." Marlee stares at her. "How did I get this lucky?"

Cadence had been practically naked last night, but Marlee didn't get to see inside her knickers—more's the pity. Now, in the lamplight, she gets to ogle that triangular patch of dark hair between her thighs in all its glory.

She's such a woman! Marlee wonders how she ever could've doubted the perfection of Cadence's naked body. Watching her approach the bed, she begins to salivate again. Will Cadence want oral sex? Should she offer? Maybe she doesn't need to. Maybe Cadence will ask her for it. Demand it even.

Cadence steps close and pulls Marlee's face against her crotch. "Do you still like the way I smell?"

Bloody hell! Where did all this sexual confidence come from? Marlee nestles her face into Cadence's mons, kissing her and smelling her.

"I love the way you smell." She grabs Cadence by the waist and pulls her onto the bed. "I can't wait to find out how you taste."

Cadence giggles, accepting a multitude of kisses on her lips, neck, stomach, and then ... Marlee stops, leaning over her, a serious question gnawing on her conscience.

"Can I ask you something, sweetheart?" Rhetorical. "What made you change your mind? The first night we spent together here, you said you weren't ready. What's different now?"

"*You* said I wasn't ready," Cadence corrects her, wrapping two limber legs around her. "*I* said I had butterflies."

"Isn't that the same thing, darling?" Marlee allows a seed of concern to take root, needing to hear that Cadence won't regret this when it's all said and done. "You were scared."

"Yeah, of being rubbish in bed." Cadence drops eye contact, admitting that as though she's ashamed to have let such a ridiculous fear get the better of her. "I was afraid I'd be awful, and then you wouldn't want me anymore."

"But, sweetheart, I—"

Cadence stifles her with a kiss, demonstrating that she's well over that brief bout of low self-esteem. "Last night, I made you come by sucking on your boob." She bursts into a grin.

"Oh, so now you think you're a stud. Is that it?" Marlee smiles down at her.

Cadence giggles again. "Hurry up and kiss me already, Marlee. I'm all tingles."

Her heart thumping, Marlee leans forward for another lip-lock. Even still, the thrill of Cadence's tongue invading her mouth an indescribable pleasure, but Cadence stops her before they make contact.

"No, not there, silly." She pushes Marlee's head south. "On my pussy." She makes herself blush just saying the word.

Dirty talk doesn't suit her. Not yet.

Smiling appreciatively—careful not to let the smile turn into a smirk—Marlee moves Cadence's legs apart and studies her young flesh. So often in the last few days, she's thought about this moment. What would Cadence look like? Would her hymen be broken already? How would she taste? Using her thumbs to open up the slippery folds of Cadence's skin, she gets the answer to her first two questions.

Cadence looks divine, her hymen perfectly intact and glistening with her arousal.

"Oh, darling. You're so beautiful."

Until this very instant, Marlee wasn't sure if the discovery of an intact hymen would be a delight or a fright. On one hand, it's a reminder of her youth and innocence—the latter of which Marlee is about to take from her, and the former she'd rather forget. On the other hand, it's symbolic of the fact that she's chosen to give herself to Marlee, and only to Marlee, which is both romantic and exciting.

So damn exciting.

Marlee runs her tongue along the length of Cadence's slit, making her twitch and buck.

Mmm, she tastes so good—so sweet.

"It tickles!" Cadence writhes.

Before laughter can take hold and potentially ruin the eroticism of the moment, Marlee holds her still, gripping her thighs firmly, and dives into her.

Immediately, Cadence's legs tense. She grunts and arches her back, her toes curling as Marlee probes and sucks her sensitive pink sex. Louder than last night, her vocalizations are throaty and deep, and it's not long before she's gyrating her hips, pushing herself into Marlee's mouth.

While thrusting upward, she brings her hand to the back of Marlee's head, demanding more pressure, and Marlee obliges as best she can. It's difficult to breathe, her face held so forcefully to the mark, but Cadence wants to be devoured, and she doesn't want to stop. She wants to make Cadence come in her mouth. She wants to feel Cadence clenching and releasing, convulsing with spasm after spasm, and it's not long before she's able to bring that sweet climax upon her with volcanic intensity.

Her orgasm is exquisite.

She shivers from head to toe, virtually screaming Marlee's name as Marlee laps her up.

"You taste delicious," Marlee whispers, kissing her inner thigh as the tremors subside.

"That was epic." Cadence sits up, leaning on her elbows to look down at Marlee between her legs. "When can I touch you? I want to make you feel the way you make me feel."

Marlee floods. Cadence wants to touch her!

Sliding off the bed, she strips—just as Cadence had done for her—baring every inch of herself. Of course, Cadence's eyes fixate on her mons, fascinated by how different it looks from her own, the light-colored hair waxed into a thin strip.

"Do you want mine to look like this?" she asks, playing with Marlee's landscaped pubic hair as they lie next to each other. "Is this better?"

"It's up to you how you want to look, darling." Marlee parts her legs. "Anything but bald. I don't want to feel as though I'm in bed with ... well, you know."

Navigating away from that awkwardness, Cadence trails her fingers down toward Marlee's cleft, slipping and sliding all over her labia.

"Wow." She grins. "You're so wet again!" She explores deeper. "And so hot!"

Marlee whines. Cadence's small hand feels so good between her legs, three slender fingers groping everything from perineum to clit. Reminding herself not to be too aggressive, she withholds from issuing demands and waits for Cadence to ask:

"Can I feel inside?"

"Yes. Oh, god, yes!" Marlee whines again, her body vibrating with anticipation.

Much slower than she would like, Cadence fumbles a finger all the way in, pushing and groping without any particular aim.

Just one finger. One slender finger.

It's not enough.

"More, darling." Marlee humps Cadence's hand. "I need you to give me more."

Cadence pushes in another keen digit. "Is this better?"

Marlee signals her approval with an affirmative growl and a thrust of her hips.

"How do I make you come?" Cadence asks then, realizing she has no real idea what to do now that they're in this position.

"Let me show you."

Marlee slips her hand over Cadence's. First, she pushes Cadence deeper, making sure she's in all the way. Then, she inserts her middle finger as well, stretching herself open wide, her palm cupping the back of Cadence's hand.

They both gasp.

"Here." She guides Cadence's fingers upward, curled to the anterior wall. "You need to find ... oh!" She jolts as Cadence's index finger touches her hidden erogenous zone.

Marlee presses Cadence's finger against the little button again. "Do you feel that, darling?"

"This?" Cadence tests by tapping it.

Marlee's pelvis jerks. "Yes!"

"What is it?" Cadence is shocked by her response to such a small gesture.

"The most sensitive part of a woman," Marlee explains, finding it difficult to concentrate on teaching instead of coming. "Keep tapping it, stroking it, and rubbing it." She pulls out to demonstrate, making a 'come hither' motion with her index and middle fingers. "See?"

"Like this?" Cadence copies her.

"Oh, fucking hell!" Marlee closes her eyes. "Just like that."

With enthusiasm and concentration, the tip of her tongue pinched between her teeth, Cadence does exactly as Marlee coaches, soon causing her experienced lover to shake uncontrollably.

"Don't stop," Marlee instructs. "Keep going." Her body starts trembling. "Yes, yes, yes! That's it!" She shudders from head to toe. "Oh, honey!"

Her last cry is quickly followed by a gush of fluid over Cadence's hand.

Neither of them expected that.

When Cadence feels the shivers subsiding, the gushing petering out, and Marlee's muscles relaxing, she extricates herself, staring down at the damp bed sheets.

"That was so strong." She examines her saturated hand. "It felt different from last time."

"It was a different kind of orgasm."

"There's more than one?"

"I thought you'd watched porn?" Marlee teases.

"It doesn't compare." Cadence licks her fingers, tasting Marlee tentatively. "I think I'd like to go down on you now," she declares, then dives south.

"Oh, damn." Marlee groans, hardly able to believe her luck as Cadence's hot mouth touches her opening for the first time.

After just a few minutes, she's close to peaking again, Cadence building her pleasure slowly but surely. Writhing on the bed, the pressure in her loins is almost

Chapter Seventeen

It's with no small amount of sadness that Marlee and Cadence pack up and leave Lymington. Oh, for just one more day. One more night. One more glorious night.

They hold hands in the chauffeur driven car, but nothing more. They steal kisses when they retreat to their rooms to unpack, and enjoy a quick, frantic grope before dinner, leaving Marlee just enough time to change back into suitable nanny attire: high heels, flowing skirt, push-up bra, and a satin blouse that was recently added to her wardrobe by Mister Ashlock. As with many of her other blouses, the buttons stop at the bust, but this one feels tighter. He probably had it made especially for her. Ugh.

Always a needlessly formal affair, dinner typically consists of Missus Ashlock asking inane questions simply for the sake of asking them, while Mister Ashlock eats in silence, glancing at Marlee's cleavage between mouthfuls. Marlee and Cadence will invariably hold up much of the table talk, sticking to topics of school, world affairs, and new music which Cadence claims Marlee will surely like if she gives it a proper chance. However, tonight's dinner is destined to take a very different turn.

"Did you have fun?" Missus Ashlock asks her daughter, enquiring about their vacation in her usual tone of not caring. "Did you try lots of new things?"

Marlee lets out an almost inaudible little squeak. Snorting as she tries to take a sip of water from her glass, she inadvertently sucks some of the liquid into her windpipe, triggering a bout of hearty, rasping coughing.

Everyone's looking at her, Cadence smirking.

"Are you quite all right?" Missus Ashlock sounds more annoyed than concerned.

"Mm-hmm." Marlee wipes tears from her eyes, composing herself. "How was your business trip?" she deflects, thinking the less their vacation is spoken of, the better.

Happy to discuss that instead, Missus Ashlock returns her gaze to her dinner. "Negotiations went well," she says offhandedly. "Contracts were signed."

Marlee doesn't like the sound of that. "Contracts, milady?"

"Cadence's marriage contract," Missus Ashlock explains casually. "Despite her rather hideous behavior at her debutante party, one of the gentlemen put in a generous offer to pair her with his son." She pauses to munch a broccoli floret. "The family will be staying with us next summer so that the children can meet one another, and their engagement will be announced at Cadence's seventeenth birthday party. They'll be married the following spring."

That all sounds painfully matter-of-fact, and entirely unemotional.

"I don't want to," Cadence protests.

"But you're going to." Missus Ashlock won't hear a word against it. "He's a lovely young man, and only a few years older than you. He speaks seven languages fluently, and is just finishing up his first bachelor's degree. You're a very lucky girl."

Lucky? Surely lucky would be getting to marry the person you're in love with?

"I'm not marrying him," Cadence insists.

"Yes, you are."

"No, I'm not."

This little back and forth argument continues for a while, emotions escalating, until Cadence blurts out something that should be game changing.

"I'm gay."

Dead silence.

Marlee chokes on a bite of her food and reaches for her glass of water to wash it down. In her periphery, she can see that Mister and Missus Ashlock aren't looking at their daughter—they're looking at *her*. Dear god, is she going to be blamed? What are they waiting for her to say? What *can* she say? Her cheeks flush.

Eventually, Missus Ashlock turns to her daughter and dismisses the declaration completely. "No, you're not." She resumes eating.

Outraged that her coming out should be so easily disregarded, Cadence slams her cutlery down on her plate. "Yes, I am!"

The clanging china makes Marlee wince, expecting that it probably heralds the commencement of war. Still, though, Mister and Missus Ashlock appear wholly unmoved.

"Didn't I tell you this would happen?" Missus Ashlock carps at her husband. "If you expose a girl to things, she starts to get ideas."

Mister Ashlock, keeping well out of this, as he usually does in family disagreements, focuses solely on his food and makes no comment.

"Don't blame Marlee!" Cadence raises her voice, her bunched up napkin following her cutlery onto the plate.

"Cadence ..." Marlee tries to call her off before any damage can be done, but it's to no avail—Cadence wants her voice heard.

"I'm gay!" She stands up so dramatically her chair tips over. "I'm not going to marry a boy! I want to be with Marlee!"

At that moment, Marlee's fairly certain her heart ceases to beat. It swells and explodes, every bit of it atomized inside her chest. Is she still breathing? She's not sure. She feels lightheaded, the world starting to tilt. Nope, she's definitely not breathing. She can't: there's no oxygen in the room. She's going to be fired. She's going to be arrested! Oh, god. She's going to go to prison!

Nope.

Yet again, Missus Ashlock surprises her.

"Of course you want to be with Marlee." She doesn't even look up from her dinner plate. "You've been clinging to her like gum on an old boot since she first set foot in this house, and being away from her is going to be awful for you, I'm sure." She shrugs. "But that's life."

"No!" Cadence starts to yell. "You're not listening!"

"I *am* listening, Cadence." The beastly woman finally looks up at her daughter. "And you know what I hear? A little girl who's having a temper tantrum because she's afraid to grow up."

Marlee's already incensed on Cadence's behalf, but Missus Ashlock isn't done hurling insults yet—there's much more to follow.

"I'm not going to let you wither away into a wretched old spinster just because you enjoy being babied by your nanny," she goes on.

Oh, how wrong she is! It's almost funny.

"Even if you did have feelings"—she sneers that word out—"for her, do you really think I'd allow you to throw away your whole future for some poverty stricken old dyke?"

Now Marlee's incensed on her own behalf, but Cadence is fighting back for both of them.

"Don't speak about Marlee like that! I love Marlee!"

Observing quietly, Marlee wonders how it's possible for a proclamation of love to feel so wonderful and yet so damn terrifying at the same time. She needn't worry, though: Missus Ashlock gives little credence to it.

126

"I'm certain you do." She returns to her food. "The same way you love Bobo, and that strange little furry creature you kept in your bedroom when you were nine."

For Cadence, the insinuation that she loves Marlee like a pet is the final straw.

"You cunt," she growls, glaring defiantly at her mother.

The vile woman snaps like a tightly wound E string. "Go to your room!"

Cadence is already halfway toward the door, which she slams on her way out.

"Impetuous little girl," Missus Ashlock mutters.

In the silence that follows, Marlee sets her knife and fork aside, rests her napkin on her plate, and politely excuses herself. "I'm sorry. I'm really not hungry anymore."

Without bothering to curtsey, she gets up from the table and leaves, deliberately avoiding eye contact with her employers. How dare Missus Ashlock speak to Cadence like that! How dare she speak about *her* like that! And to do so with such a callous disregard for either of their feelings. What a repugnant human being!

Marlee's had enough. From now on, the only thing that matters is loving Cadence.

To hell with everything else.

ON HER WAY UP THE MAIN STAIRCASE, MARLEE MAKES A swift decision about what to do next: she's going to make love to Cadence. Fuck the Ashlocks. She and Cadence are going to have sex in their house, while they're home, and she's not going to feel guilty about it in the least.

Battling tears of anger, she goes straight to Cadence's bedroom and knocks on the door.

There's no answer.

She enters anyway, checking to see if Cadence is anywhere inside, but she's not.

Damn.

Perhaps she's in the games room crying, and perhaps that's for the best.

Marlee inhales deeply and gathers herself. Shagging while the Ashlocks are in such close range would be needlessly risky, so she convinces herself it was nothing more than a ridiculously hotheaded thought that's probably best forgotten.

Taking a moment to calm herself, she slips through the open cheater door into her own room, prepared instead to lie on her bed and stare aimlessly at the ceiling, or weep, but ...

Cadence is lying naked on the bed, the duvet discarded on the floor. She's on her stomach, legs bent at the knees, ankles crossed, long chestnut hair spilling over her bare back and shoulders, cascading onto the bed.

"Oh, heavens." Marlee clutches her chest, her exclamation of happy surprise immediately followed by a reflexive chastisement that carries no emotion whatsoever. "You shouldn't be in here."

"It's too late to try and nanny me now, Marlee." Cadence smirks, feet wiggling gleefully.

She's right. Marlee has absolutely no hope of commanding her to do anything ever again; the authority she had over this child is long gone. The best she can hope for now is that Cadence will have the maturity to behave properly without being prompted, or will simply comply with her requests out of love, not necessity.

Of course, there's always the possibility that was the only reason she was ever so well behaved in the first place: to please her nanny. Perhaps the authority was merely an illusion from the outset. Perhaps it was love's influence all along.

"I think it's about time I issued *you* some orders for a change," Cadence continues, tapping her index finger against her lower lip, feigning deep thought on the matter. "Now get over here and touch me." She beckons to Marlee with the same 'come hither' fingers she used to bring on her climax yesterday.

Smiling, arousal returning, Marlee obeys willingly. "You were very brave this evening, darling," she says, sitting on the edge of the bed and slipping out of her heels. "It took a lot of courage to tell your parents how you feel about me."

"They didn't listen." Cadence sulks, picking at a split end in her hair.

"That's not so important right now." Marlee hitches up her skirt and moves closer. "What matters is that you said it. You told the truth, whether they want to believe it or not."

"But what good does it do if they won't pay any attention to me?"

She has a point.

Still, Marlee doesn't want her to waste precious time worrying about something that's completely out of their control.

"Sshhh. Let's not talk about this anymore. Not tonight." She kisses Cadence's head. "If your parents won't reconsider your match, I'll have to think of something."

"You will?" Cadence sounds mostly hopeful, only mildly skeptical.

Marlee moves Cadence's tresses off her shoulders and back, baring her skin for kisses. "I won't let them marry you off to someone else without a fight."

Waving goodbye to any concerns still lingering in the back of her mind about being caught diddling the Ashlocks' daughter, Marlee settles herself behind Cadence, stroking and kissing her bare back and rump. The curve of her spine is so wonderfully sensual, ending with two little dimples just above her bum.

Mmm, her naked bum.

Marlee can't resist. She brings a flat palm down against one of Cadence's butt cheeks.

Slap!

Cadence squeals.

Marlee grabs her muscular ass. "You have such an incredible bum."

"Spank me again." Cadence angles her butt upwards.

Complying willingly, Marlee brings a palm down on her cheek again, slightly harder this time, leaving behind a pink handprint.

"That stings." Cadence pretends to be upset, looking at Marlee over her shoulder. "Now you have to kiss it better."

Marlee leans forward, kisses her, then bites her, eliciting another squeal.

"I love you, Marlee." Cadence waggles her bum, encouraging more kisses and caresses, her spirits lifted. "I don't ever want this to end."

"Me neither, sweetheart."

Though she wants to ignore it, Cadence detects a hint of sorrow in Marlee's voice, as if the end, however unwanted, is sadly inevitable and unavoidable. Is she capitulating before the fight even begins? Resigning herself to failure?

"I have an idea," she volunteers cautiously. "What if *you* marry me? They can't marry me off if I'm already wedded to someone else."

Marlee's ministrations stop abruptly, her breath caught in her throat.

After a while, "What's the matter, Marlee?" Cadence turns her attention back to the split end, her mood subdued by Marlee's apparent reticence. "You don't want to?"

Marlee leans forward, pressing her cheek to Cadence's back, holding the young teen. Closing her eyes, she squeezes a handful of tears loose, the salty droplets forming a narrow rivulet from Cadence's shoulder blades, puddling at the small of her back.

Oh, the thought! The thought of making a life with Cadence is positively electrifying, but even if it were possible, the last thing Marlee wants is for Cadence to feel as though she's evading one marriage only to be flung headfirst into another. Focusing on that, she cools the teen's enthusiasm, softening the rejection with a healthy dose of reality.

"You need parental consent to marry before you're eighteen, darling."

"Not everywhere," Cadence murmurs, her confidence knocked. "Not in Scotland. The age is sixteen there—I checked." She rests her chin on her arms, not daring to roll over and look Marlee in the eye. "I thought we could go there next summer, for the last long weekend we'll get to spend together. I'll have finished school by then. There'll be nothing holding me here."

Shocked by Cadence's unflinching devotion to her, Marlee hesitates to respond. Matrimony is one heck of a commitment for a sixteen-year-old to contemplate, never mind for a seventeen-year-old to

132

undertake. But then, an arranged marriage is one hell of a burden for a girl of any age to be lumbered with.

Eventually, "You're so young." Marlee nuzzles her hair. "This is all terribly unfair on you."

Cadence shakes her head. "I've been raised for marriage, Marlee. Like geese who grow up on a farm, only to be cooked for dinner. They're born for the purpose of being eaten, and I was born just so I could be married and sent away." Her voice cracks, but she doesn't cry.

"Oh, darling." Marlee kisses her head. "Your parents don't deserve you."

"They don't want me." Cadence arches her back, pushing her bum up against Marlee. "You're the only person who's ever wanted me." She rests on her elbows, peering over her shoulder. "You do want me, don't you, Marlee?"

"What do you think?" Marlee grabs Cadence's hips and raises them, bringing her to her knees so that she can reach around and touch between her legs. "Do you want me to show you?"

She pushes a finger inside, seeking out that deep place, but finds it difficult to get at from this angle. She tries to edge a second finger in, but feels Cadence tense up so she stops.

It's so hard not to give her more.

It's so hard not to fuck her.

Cadence moves her body perfectly, adapting to Marlee's rhythm, changing the angle of her hips to better enable deep penetration, or to make sure Marlee hits certain areas that feel good. How did she ever learn to be this sexy? How did she learn to move in such a way? Marlee suspects it's to do with porn, although that's not really of any importance. What matters is that she's hungry for intimacy, eager to explore new sensations, and she wants to please as much as she wants to *be* pleased. She's perfection.

It's such a relief, too. In the past, Marlee's been with some sexually experienced women who thought their part in lovemaking involved little more than lying on their backs with their legs open. She's so glad Cadence isn't a lazy or complacent lover—this bodes well for the future. *Their* future, which she's ever more determined they'll have.

She starts to thrust rhythmically inside her young lover. In her own vagina—used to the penetration of dildos and multiple fingers—she can barely register the movement of one finger slipping in and out, and gets little pleasure from it. That's not the case for Cadence, though. In her tight body—the walls of her inner sex swollen with arousal, the muscles clamping down—the gentle plunge of one finger is definitely enough.

Cadence whimpers. "Do you like making love to me, Marlee?"

Marlee is overwhelmed. Cadence's deliciously firm ass is raised, grinding against her, rocking back and forth. She's leaning on her elbows, her chest angled down, cheek pressed against the pillow. Who saw this coming two weeks ago? Bending forward, Marlee presses her breasts against Cadence's back, leaning over her, pushing deep inside her.

"Say my name again."

"Mmmmarlee," Cadence coos, drawing a murmur of pleasure into her name.

"Louder," Marlee demands.

"Don't we have to be quiet?"

"I don't care." Marlee finds Cadence's g-spot.

"Oh!" Cadence cries out, grabbing a fistful of pillow. "Marlee!"

"I'm going to make you come the way you made me come last night." Marlee targets the hidden button of skin relentlessly. "Do you want that?"

"Yessssssss!" Her muscles clench, gripping Marlee's fingers like a vise. "Make me come! Oh, god, Marlee! Make me come!"

She does, and it's loud.

If anyone happened to be walking by the bedroom, they'd easily hear. And Marlee's long past caring.

Chapter Nineteen

A BREEZE DRIFTING IN FROM THE OPEN WINDOW LIFTS the hem of Marlee's skirt, exposing a stockinged thigh. Taking advantage of the enticement, Cadence glides a hand under the skirt, finding the top of the stocking and the smooth skin beyond.

"That was so epic." She relaxes on Marlee's chest. "But how come it wasn't messy? Like it was with you."

"Not every woman comes like that, and not necessarily every time." Marlee kisses the top of her head, allaying her concerns. "Every orgasm is unique."

Cadence ponders that for a while, leading her to wonder about the breadth of Marlee's past experiences. "Have you ever had an orgasm with a fella?"

"No," Marlee answers softly, getting a sense of where this conversation's about to go long before it gets there. "Why do you ask?"

It takes Cadence a while to articulate herself, feeling unnecessarily embarrassed by the topic, and when she does finally speak, her voice has a slight tremor to it, all self-assurance evaporated.

"What does it feel like to have a ... a thing inside you?"

She grimaces at the word 'thing', and Marlee feels a small shudder run through her.

"It depends." Marlee twists around to face her. "Some women like penetration, others don't. It doesn't matter whether you're gay or straight, it's all about what makes you feel good."

Cadence digests that, applying this new information to the sensations and passions she's feeling. "In that case, I think I want more." Some of her confidence returns. "I want you inside me, but deeper. More than just fingers. Does that make sense?" She doesn't wait for Marlee to answer. "I want you to fill me, and be in every inch of me. Is that terribly dirty?"

Terribly, delightfully dirty, Marlee thinks, excited by the thought of taking Cadence that way. But does Cadence really know what she's asking for? Is that really what she wants? Phallic penetration? Are they even on the same page?

"Are you saying you want us to make love the way heterosexual couples do?" she asks in the most delicate way possible, just in case she's misinterpreting Cadence's craving.

"I think so." Cadence rolls over and looks up at her. "Can we do that?" She quirks an impish grin. "I want to try it with you."

As much as Marlee is eager to say yes and reach for the bedside table, she has to admit that she's conflicted and concerned. She was hoping to have a little more time to ease Cadence into this kind of lovemaking—assuming she'd want it at all—and she has no idea how her snug body will accommodate something of such girth. Nevertheless, she's keen to further their newly flowering physical relationship, and she certainly doesn't want to deny Cadence something that might bring her incredible satisfaction.

Thus, "Of course, sweetheart. We can make love any way you want, but you're so tight and I don't want to hurt you. Are you sure you wouldn't rather wait a while?"

"I want you in every way, Marlee." Cadence peels away from her, sprawling naked on the bed, legs spread and back arched, breasts bouncing. "I'm certain of it."

After doing away with her clothing, Marlee reaches for the drawer in the bedside table and pulls out an L-shaped, silicone dildo. It's eight inches of cock, with a contoured bulb 'handle' that enables both partners to gain pleasure from it without needing to be strapped into an uncomfortable, bulky harness.

At first sight of it, Cadence's eyes widen, almost aghast. "It's so big!" she exclaims. "How will it fit?"

"It might hurt at first," Marlee concedes, that being her fear from the outset.

Cadence looks worried, her brow puckered with concern and confusion. "But it doesn't hurt when you use your fingers."

"Finger," Marlee disillusions her, setting the dildo on the bedside table. "You're very tight, and I've been very gentle. Your body's still quite virginal."

"How come?" Cadence's frown deepens.

"Young girls have a kind of barrier inside them," Marlee explains delicately. "It's a protective membrane that gets broken when the girl has penetrative sex for the first time, and—"

"A hymen, Marlee." Cadence rolls her eyes. "You can say hymen. I'm not retarded."

Marlee scowls. "Fine. If you know what it is, why did you ask?"

"Because I thought you ... when you ... and then we ... oh ..."

Suddenly, she seems so lost and small. Vulnerable even. She hasn't been made a woman in the way she thought she had, and that saddens her beyond words, as though she's been cheated out of something special.

Marlee gets it.

She bends forward and kisses her, explaining gently, "We've still had sex, honey. We've had amazing, wonderful sex, I just haven't broken you in. Not completely. I've stretched you a little, but I didn't want to tear you. Just in case."

"Just in case what?"

That's a good question, and Marlee can't think of an answer that doesn't sound utterly ridiculous. Just in case she has to take a husband? Just in case he checks? Gawd, who pays attention to that sort of thing anymore? No-one. Most girls break their hymens long before they have intercourse for the first time. Even if a new husband should notice she'd been breached, he wouldn't likely leap to the conclusion that she'd taken another lover between her legs. It could've happened horseback riding, or with the use of tampons, or gymnastics, or masturbation, or any number of other things. Whoever would suspect that the nanny was to blame?

Honestly, she'd even been a little surprised to gaze upon that perfect, unbroken membrane of light pink skin, staggered to find it completely intact. Staggered and excited. Excited and terrified.

She'd positively vibrated with the thought of being the one to break through that last vestige of childhood and bring her darling Cadence fully into womanhood. But at the same time, she hadn't been able to overlook the magnitude of the responsibility. Hadn't been able to overlook it, nor come to terms with it—and that's the crux of the issue, she realizes.

Keeping Cadence's hymen intact gave her a convenient mental loophole, and plausible deniability. In that way, Cadence was still just as innocent as she always had been, and nothing was lost. They could touch and caress, and bring each other mutual satisfaction without having to sacrifice her purity.

How illogical! The very moment she trailed her hand between Cadence's legs and felt the folds of her most private place, all innocence was lost. She'd made love to Cadence, and whether her hymen was broken or not didn't matter, they'd still done the deed. Multiple times.

"I know my concerns are silly, and dreadfully old fashioned," Marlee confesses, reaching down and pushing one careful finger into Cadence's wetness. "I'm so paranoid someone will find out what we've begun doing, that's all."

Cadence's body yields smoothly to Marlee's penetration, the walls of her inner sex offering little resistance.

"More," she begs almost immediately, just as Marlee had done in the Lymington bed and breakfast. "I need more."

Marlee smiles, aware that Cadence is using her as a behavioral template. "You know I'm not even supposed to talk about these things with you, much less *do* them. This is so naughty."

She pulls her finger all the way out, presses her index and middle fingers together, then teases them back in, millimeter by millimeter, just the tips at first.

Cadence holds her breath, and Marlee feels her body clench, clamping down on her. She eases in another inch, then Cadence winces.

"Too much." She squirms.

"Relax." Marlee tenders her a kiss. "Let me make love to you."

After a few more kisses, Cadence's muscles loosen and Marlee slips her fingers all the way in, reaching deep inside.

"How does that feel?" She strokes Cadence's spongy ridges.

"Better." Cadence lifts her knees, giving Marlee better access. "Nice."

Marlee keeps going, coaxing Cadence's orgasm to the surface. When she feels Cadence is getting close, she pushes even deeper, going above and beyond that most sensitive place.

"How about now?"

All Cadence can muster in response is a faint peep between fast, shallow breaths. Marlee can feel her body teetering on the fringe of climax, her legs beginning to twitch, and she so wants to tip her over the edge. Wriggling lower, she sucks Cadence's clit into her mouth, bringing on a climax that erupts suddenly and powerfully—and loudly.

"That hurt, Marlee." Tears well in Cadence's downturned eyes.

"Oh, darling." Marlee peppers her lips with kisses. "If you want to stop—"

"No!" Cadence is quite resolute, reaching for Marlee's bum, pulling her closer. "Keep going. I want to do this with you. Please!"

After breaking through Cadence's hymen, Marlee slides the rest of the shaft deep into her sex without much effort, bumping up against her rubbery cervix. When she's in all the way, she lies perfectly still, kissing Cadence's soft lips.

"There." She grips Cadence's bum and lifts her hips off the bed, impaling her firmly but gently. "How's that?"

"Feels so big." Cadence wraps her legs around Marlee's waist, her eyes closed, savoring this new sensation inside her. "So full."

"Is that what you were craving?"

"Uh-huh." Cadence nods, undulating her pelvis against Marlee, making the cock move inside her. "Feels perfect."

Encouraged by her movements, Marlee very slowly withdraws almost to the tip of the cock, then rocks back in up to the hilt. She's rewarded with a drawn out purr, followed by a breathy whisper.

"Yesssssssss!" Cadence flings her arms around Marlee's neck.

Marlee moves a little faster and a little harder, discovering as she does that phallic penetration makes Cadence very vocal. Damn, that's sexy.

Occasionally, Cadence winces, but the sharp creases of pain on her brow quickly fade, soon replaced by waves of pleasure. Eventually, another orgasm announces its arrival with a quiver that runs from her head to her toes, making them curl, and she throws her head back, her whole body—inside and out—soon overtaken by spasms.

As the crest rolls over her, Marlee rests on top of her, sighing contentedly into the pillow, careful not to put too much weight on her chest. She's tired, out of breath, but so very happy.

"Marlee." Cadence nudges her.

All Marlee can manage in response is a faint, satisfied murmur.

"Marlee, Marlee, Marlee." Cadence wriggles playfully, determined to elicit a response.

Marlee murmurs again. "Yes, darling?"

"When can we do that again?" She's beaming. "Can I do it to you?"

Wow. This is bliss, Marlee thinks.

Pure, unadulterated bliss.

Chapter Twenty

DESPITE FREQUENT DILDO SLIPPAGES AND SOME POOR coordination, being penetrated by Cadence feels phenomenal. Already brought to the brink of climax when she was the one on top, Marlee has her first orgasm within seconds of Cadence's entry into her sex. Her next comes ten minutes later, when Cadence finally manages to hold a rhythm.

"That's it, darling," Marlee cheers her on. "That's ... just ... unghh."

Her words dissolve to grunts and groans, and she convulses around the dildo, her muscles clenching it so tightly that when Cadence pulls back, it gets left behind.

"Oops." Cadence pants, peeking down between their legs. "I lost it again."

"It's okay." Marlee chuckles, letting her roll off and onto the bed, depositing the sticky, slippery dildo on the floor. "You got the job done."

"My arse hurts." Cadence flops into the sheets, her thighs burning from the exertion. "And my legs are all wibbly-wobbly."

"It takes some getting used to." Marlee gives her a quick kiss, then pulls the duvet up and settles next to her, an arm and a leg flung over her.

"I *am* gay, Marlee," Cadence says then, completely out of the blue. "I've been thinking about it a lot, and I really don't like the thought of being with a boy at all."

"Have you ever been close to any of the boys at your school?" Marlee wonders.

Cadence shakes her head. "I've been asked out a couple of times. I even said yes once."

"How old were you?"

"Thirteen. It was just before you came to work here. He asked me to go to a movie with him, and I kinda wanted to see it, so I went. He was holding my hand, and I think he was nervous 'cause his palm was all sweaty. Then he put my hand in his lap and ... he had ... you know, a stiffie. I was curious, so I touched it. It didn't feel like much, but I knew some of my friends were tossing off their boyfriends and stuff, so I thought I'd give it a go."

Though Cadence had openly confessed to never having been touched or kissed, Marlee hadn't before considered the possibility that she might've had other kinds of exploratory sexual experiences with her peers.

"You wanked him in the cinema?" She tries not to sound too surprised.

"Yeah, kind of," Cadence confesses shyly. "I put my hand in his trousers, wrapped my fingers around it, and just sort of ..." She pantomimes a pumping motion with her wrist, her fingers curled around an invisible stick. "Then, all of a sudden, it just ..." She pantomimes an explosion.

Marlee laughs, rolling onto her back.

Cadence sits up to look at her. "It was so disgusting." She pulls a face. "I can't even begin to tell you how awful it felt. It was all over my hand."

"What did you do with the mess?" Marlee's still laughing.

"I wiped it on the seat in front." Cadence glances at the open palm of her right hand, as if it's forever tainted. "I had to get it off me, and there was nowhere else." The disgusted grimace dissolves into a frown of worry. "Do you think I'm filthy?"

Marlee's laughter ebbs away. "No, darling. It's perfectly normal."

"It didn't feel normal." Cadence snuggles back down, her naked breasts smooshed against Marlee's ribcage. "I thought there must be something wrong with me."

Concerned, Marlee rolls her over, leaning above her. "Why, love?"

Cadence shrugs, goose bumps pricking her naked skin as a breeze whispers through the room. "It didn't make me feel the way my friends said it would."

"Ah, I know how that goes." Marlee's lips curve upward, referencing the memory banks from her late teens, and every first date since then. "You were hoping for butterflies? Your heart pounding? Palms sweaty? An indescribable heat between your legs?" She trails a fingertip over Cadence's taut stomach, causing more goose bumps to appear.

"I didn't feel like that until I met you." Cadence looks up at her, tucking her golden mane behind her ears. "I thought you were the most beautiful thing I'd ever seen."

"Charmer." Marlee pokes her ribs playfully.

"It's true," Cadence insists, dropping her gaze. "But I bet you only saw a little kid."

To spare Cadence's feelings and boost her ego, Marlee really wishes she could say otherwise, but she won't lie. Besides, the honest truth isn't completely innocent.

"Mostly," she ends up admitting vaguely.

Cadence's eyes flit back to hers, urging her to expound.

"You've always been tall for your age," Marlee continues. "You didn't exactly look thirteen when we met. I mean, you weren't a woman, obviously, but you certainly weren't a little girl." She caresses Cadence's naked form beneath the covers. "Over the last few years, you've been growing up right in front of me, and I haven't been oblivious. Not to your development, nor to the way you've always looked at me."

"You never said anything."

"What was there to say?" Marlee shrugs. "My first teenage crush was my French teacher—it's not unusual. I assumed it would pass, and saw no point in embarrassing you by acknowledging it, even when you started trying to flirt with me."

"I did not!" Cadence blushes, giving Marlee's shoulder a light smack.

"Oh, please!" Marlee rolls her eyes. "Remember that school field trip to Bournemouth last semester? You were leaning on the railing, looking out over the ocean, and I was behind you, resting my chin on your head. You arched your back and stuck your rump right out at me. If you'd have been a little taller, your derrière would've been grinding into my crotch." The memory makes her laugh. "And then there was that time you came out of the pool and dumped water all over me while I was half asleep on a sun lounger."

"I was cooling you off!"

"And I'm sure it was a total coincidence that I was wearing a white cotton blouse that day? I didn't realize how translucent everything was until I went upstairs to change. Honestly, Cady, you could see *everything*."

"I guess my technique wasn't so smooth, huh?" Cadence concedes that she might have a lot to learn in the art of flirtation. "I just wanted you to notice me in a different way."

"I noticed you." Marlee caresses her face. "I shouldn't have, but I did, and now that we're here, I want you know that I'll do anything in my power to prevent whatever marriage your parents intend to arrange for you."

"Anything?" Cadence grins, fidgeting excitedly, full to the brim with restless energy. "Scotland and all?"

Marlee nods. "I wish we didn't have to rush everything along so fast, but quite apart from what's developed between you and I, I can't bear the thought of your parents tossing you into a man's bed if what you really want is to be in a woman's."

"Good." Cadence flips her over and straddles her. "Because I don't want to marry some smelly boy. I want to marry *you*."

Every cell in Marlee's body vibrates with yearning. Hearing Cadence express the desire for marriage outright, completely separated from the messy business of escaping the clutches of another, is incredibly exhilarating.

"Do you really mean that, love?"

"Of course I mean it." Cadence laughs, amused that Marlee should have to ask. "I've never wanted to be with anyone else. Only you. Forever."

"But it means giving up everything. Do you understand that? Your parents could disinherit you."

Cadence shrugs. "I don't care. What's this money ever done for me? Isolated me, confined me, and made me miserable."

"And allowed you to wear the finest clothes, ride horses, go on international vacations"—Marlee counts the benefits off on her fingers—"attend an excellent private school, and—"

"Hey!" Cadence puts a hand over her mouth, silencing her. "I prefer wearing my shitty old jeans and t-shirts than all that posh gear, I only ever go riding because I like looking at you in your riding outfit, I don't much care for exotic beaches and scorching weather, and I hate my stupid school."

Marlee peels her hand away. "Don't lie about your school; you've made lots of friends there. Anyhow, the point I was trying to make is that I don't have any money. I think I might have enough saved for a down payment on a house, but that's about it."

"So?" Cadence shrugs again.

"I can't afford diamonds."

"I'm not bothered about diamonds."

"I can't support you." Marlee winces apologetically, as if afraid that the reality of the situation might cause Cadence to come to her senses. "If you seriously want to be with me away from this house, you'll need to get a job."

"I know." Cadence takes Marlee's hand, sensing her apprehension. "I'm not opposed to hard work, Marl. As long as we have each other, everything will be all right."

Marlee smiles. She's never heard Cadence shorten her name like that before, and she basks in it. It's such a small thing, yet it feels like the next stage in the evolution of their relationship: an extra layer of familiarity. And by this time next year, they could be a legally wedded couple.

Oh, the thought!

Chapter Twenty-one

FROM THAT DAY FORWARD, SEX BECOMES A REGULAR part of their relationship. Almost a full year passes, Cadence finishes her compulsory education, and by the time she's a day away from her seventeenth birthday, they're making love multiple times daily. Cadence hasn't spent a single night in her own bed since she—rather unsuccessfully—came out to her parents, and no-one's noticed how she and Marlee are practically living as a couple in this expansive house, virtually ignored as they are by the other residents.

If anyone's ever overheard their exuberant and frequent lovemaking, it's never been mentioned or questioned, yet neither of them do much to hide it. Just this morning, Marlee was crying out with Cadence on top of her, impaling her with all eight inches of the dildo.

Her insides still throbbing, she fluffs the pillow under her head and turns away from the glare of the sunlight streaming in through the window. Damn, it feels good to be fucked by Cadence. She has so much stamina—a testament to her athleticism—and the thrust of her hips is so powerful, and so unrelenting. It's hard to believe she's still only sixteen years old. Harder still to believe that, not so long ago, she was an innocent virgin, experiencing her first real orgasm, scared to initiate adult intimacy even though she clearly wanted it.

Marlee chuckles to herself. Sixteen years old! Seventeen in less than twenty-four hours, but still: so young, and yet so proficient. Their lovemaking is exhausting, Cadence being so energetic, insatiable, and demanding. If Marlee had to get up and run for her life right now, she doubts that she could. Her legs are like jelly: weak, and utterly incapable of carrying her weight anywhere—even to the bathroom.

She's had to pee for the last ten minutes, but she's forcing her bladder to hold it. Besides, Cadence is in the bathroom showering. Isn't she? Wait. The sound of running water's stopped. As she registers that, the duvet is suddenly yanked down and a naked crotch is pressed against her bare bum, straddling her.

"Are you awake, Marlee?"

Cadence's voice is so warm and sultry, her hands roaming from shoulders to lower back, sodden hair dripping. Does she want to go at it again? Why not? It's been all of half an hour.

Marlee wriggles onto her back, yawning as she looks up at her eager, naked lover's breasts, her slender waist, perfectly proportioned hips, and the small strip of dark curly hair leading down to her core.

Before offering her any encouragement, Marlee checks the bedside clock. "I don't know that we have enough time for this, darling. We should get going."

"Where?"

"Shopping." Marlee reaches up and fondles Cadence's breasts. "We need to buy you a new dress."

"Why?" Cadence's lips turn pouty, her smile fading. "I have plenty of dresses."

"Yes"—Marlee massages two swelling nipples— "but your parents want you in something new for your birthday party tomorrow."

"My engagement party, you mean." Her thirst for some more hanky panky subdued, Cadence pulls Marlee's hands away. "I don't even want to have this stupid party. I wish we could call the whole thing off and just—"

Marlee puts a finger to her lips. "The party has to go ahead, so you may as well enjoy it."

"How can I?" Cadence bats her hand away.

"Because we'll be there together." Marlee drives a hand between Cadence's legs, thrusting two fingers all the way inside her without hesitation or delicacy. "We'll celebrate your birthday, then we'll be off on a train to Scotland. We'll be married."

Cadence plants her hands on Marlee's naked breasts and starts to ride her fingers, simulating phallic coitus, the desire for a quick, firm fuck engulfing her in seconds. She certainly isn't a virgin anymore! Her body's grown accustomed to penetration, allowing Marlee to relax completely when they make love, no longer having to worry about using too much force and accidentally tearing her. Not only that, but in the last twelve months, she's started to take control of her sexual needs. She's become keenly aware of what she likes, what she wants, and how to maximize her pleasure. To that end, she stops moving and fumbles to open the drawer in the bedside table.

"I need you this way," she says, grabbing the dildo and easing the bulb inside Marlee.

Happy to oblige, Marlee extracts her fingers and watches Cadence angle the head of the cock between her legs. She presses it into her wet flesh and slides herself down over the shaft, taking it deep without any difficulty.

How erotic that is still, to watch the shaft disappear inside her, swallowed up by her hungry sex. More erotic even than the first time, when Marlee was so worried about causing her pain. Breaking her in was exhilarating, the illicit thrill of it so arousing, but making love to her like this—to see how self-assured and capable she is as a lover—is a pleasure beyond any measure.

She pushes up into her, and at that moment, there's a sharp knock against Cadence's bedroom door. Shit. Has someone finally heard them?

"Who the hell could that be?" Cadence crabs, slumping against Marlee's chest.

After a moment's thought, Marlee suspects she knows exactly who it is: Vincent Cartwright, otherwise known as Cadence's future husband. He and his family are staying with them to celebrate Cadence's birthday. Or more accurately, to formally announce the Ashlock-Cartwright engagement.

Another round of knocks spurs Cadence to act.

"Hold on," she calls out, uncoupling herself from Marlee.

While she grabs a bathrobe and disappears through the open cheater door into her old room, Marlee sets the dildo aside and gets out of bed, dressing as quickly as she can. God, she hopes he didn't hear!

Keeping as quiet as possible, she pricks her ears and listens as Cadence opens the door to a twenty-year-old boy with blue eyes and a head of thick, dark hair.

In pristine, newly shined leather shoes, pressed trousers, and a crisp white dress shirt, he doesn't look his age at all. He should be wearing torn jeans, sneakers, and an over-washed t-shirt, but he's not interested in that. He wants to look like a man. He wants to behave like a man. Or at least, his perception of what a man ought to be.

"What do you want?" Cadence snaps at him.

"I'm heading up to the games room." He takes in her appearance. "I thought you might like to join me."

"No." Cadence tries to shut the door, but he stops it with his foot.

"Have you seen the maid?" he asks boldly, peeking into the room. "I've looked everywhere for her, but I can't seem to find her."

"Who? Marlee? Marlee isn't a maid." Cadence forces the door closed slightly, limiting his view. "And you have no right to request her."

152

"I'm a guest in your house, Cadence." He smiles smugly, stuffing both hands in his pockets. "I have a right to see my needs tended to."

"Sure you do, but not by Marlee."

Afraid that Cadence's tongue will start to get away from her—which it's very apt to do—Marlee walks in from the other bedroom, tucking her blouse into her skirt. Unbeknownst to her, she's missed fastening the top button, leaving her bra exposed.

"Is there something you need, Master Cartwright?" She appears at Cadence's shoulder.

Vince eyes her bosom. At first, she assumes he's being a typical young boy—her nanny outfits are quite revealing—but then she looks down and finds herself indecent. Without making too much out of it, she swiftly buttons herself up.

"Master Cartwright," she prompts him. "Do you require assistance of some kind?"

"Quite urgently." His gaze diverts to her eyes. "I requested fresh towels daily, and I've yet to receive any this morning."

"My apologies, sir." Marlee dips her head subserviently, but has no discernible hint of emotion in her voice. "Allow me to see to that immediately."

She takes a step toward the door, but Cadence puts an arm out, blocking her way.

"Marlee's not a dog." She glares at Vince. "And she certainly does not respond to your call."

Marlee stifles a gasp, shocked by the physical response Cadence's recently emerging protective streak stirs in her knickers. It seems the older Cadence gets, and the closer they become to one another, the less the ballsy teen's able to tolerate any slight or disrespect aimed in her direction—and it excites her. Cadence is growing into such a strong young woman.

"Forgive me"—Vince is pushy and undeterred, targeting Cadence with steely eyes—"but Marlee is an employee of this house, is she not?"

"For now, but not for much longer, and she tends only to me. If you need something, you may ring the bell and ask for Rachel. She'll see to you." Cadence slams the door on him, her expression full of loathing as she turns to face Marlee. "He's such a dick. He shouldn't speak to you like that."

"Still, he's the boy your mother wishes you to marry." Marlee feigns seriousness. "Don't you think you should treat him with some modicum of respect?"

They erupt in laughter.

"Shit." Cadence stifles herself abruptly, entertaining the same horrifying thought that crossed Marlee's mind a few minutes ago. "Do you think he heard us having sex?"

"I don't know." Marlee glides her hands around Cadence's slender waist and pushes her up against the door, planting kisses on her. "But we'll have to be very careful for the next two days. You know that, don't you? We might not get much time together."

"We must," Cadence insists adamantly, miserably contemplating spending her birthday celebrations wound up with unfulfilled sexual longings. "If I don't get to make love with you at least once a day, I'll go bat shit crazy."

Marlee smirks. A girl who's technically not yet old enough to be with her at all is making sexual demands! Her heart pitter-patters.

"Come on, let's go." She drags Cadence back into her bedroom. "I'm eager to watch you try on sexy dresses. It might be the only enjoyment I get all day."

Chapter Twenty-two

WATCHING CADENCE PERUSE A LINGERIE RACK IN THE fifth clothing store they've visited thus far, Marlee's mind races back twelve months, remembering the first time they found themselves in this position. Then, the hand holding was purely platonic. Today, it's anything but. Then, it was a black lace bra that caught Cadence's attention. Today, it's a red lace bra with a velvet heart pattern—matching knickers, too.

They would look incredible on her.

"I think we're becoming distracted." Marlee tries to turn her in the direction of the eveningwear section. "Dresses are this way."

"But it's my birthday tomorrow." Cadence juts out her bottom lip. "Wouldn't you like me to wear something sexy on my birthday?"

"Yes, which is why I want you to come with me and pick out a dress."

Marlee takes her by the hand and leads her over to the appropriate section, but that doesn't make Cadence any less distracted. She's been stealing less-than-subtle glances at Marlee's cleavage since they left the house, and Marlee can't take much more of it. She notices every time Cadence's soft eyes wander, landing upon the generous 'V' shown off by the open neckline of her blouse, and she feels her nipples harden.

Concealed by racks of clothing, she slides behind Cadence, embracing her.

"You're staring."

"Am I?" Cadence pretends to be clueless.

"You are. You keep looking at my chest."

"What's the matter?" Cadence teases. "You don't like it when I look at you?"

"I love it when you look at me, but you have to control yourself when we're out. We both do." Marlee rubs her waist. "We could still get into a lot of trouble for loving one another the way we do. We're not quite out of the woods yet."

Knowing just what to say to make Marlee weak, Cadence turns her head to the side and whispers, "I ache when I look at you."

She's grown to be an expert at baiting that hook and tossing it in the water.

"Where?" Marlee bites on the line without hesitation, quickly making sure no-one's looking before she reaches for one of Cadence's breasts. "Here?" She fondles it.

"Yessssssss." Cadence leans into her.

Marlee coaxes her nipple stiff, then forces herself to stop. By the letter of the law, Cadence is still a child in her care. A sexually precocious, beautiful, irresistible child.

"That's enough, darling." She disengages her hand.

"But now you've made me all tingly," Cadence complains. "You're so cruel."

"Behave." Marlee gives her bum a brief pat as she pulls away.

Cadence manages to follow that instruction for the better part of half an hour, during which time she tries on and rejects six different dresses that manage to generate a whole range of responses from Marlee.

"Oh, no, darling." Vigorous head shaking. "Not that one."

"Ooh, that's adorable." Wink.

"Meh." Shrug.

"I like it." Noncommittal.

"That color does nothing for your beautiful eyes, sweetheart."

"That's nice." Head cocked to the side, admiring her ass.

This time, there's no pretence that Cadence is selecting a dress based purely on Marlee's reaction to it, and Marlee feels quite comfortable offering her honest opinions. When Cadence gets to the seventh dress out of the nine possibilities she took with her into the changing room, however, she's after more than just a compliment. Dress on, she opens the door, peeks her head out, and calls for Marlee.

"Psst, Marlee." She beckons her inside. "I need your help."

Suspecting a trick, but powerless to resist anyway, Marlee gets up off the comfy chair she's been lounging on for half an hour, hopes none of the sales staff are watching, and joins Cadence in the tiny cubicle. There's not enough room to swing a cat inside the cluttered box, so even if Cadence is up to something wayward, there's going to be a limit to what they can accomplish in such a small space.

Dresses are crumpled on the floor in an array of colors. Cadence is wearing a lined, white satin, above-the-knee dress, sleeveless, with an empire waist. It has a black silk sash around the middle, decorated with black beading, and she looks like a princess.

"You like?" She grabs the hem and lifts it higher, revealing more thigh.

Marlee takes a half-step closer. "We shouldn't be doing this."

"No?" Cadence reaches between her own legs, draws her fingers along the drenched flesh between her thighs, then holds them up, slick with moisture. "But it's really wet down there."

Overcome, Marlee grabs Cadence by the hips and pushes her back, shoving her forcefully against the changing room wall, making her squeal with delight.

"You're so naughty." She snatches Cadence's wrist and sucks her sticky fingers clean, tasting her abundant arousal. "And yummy." She reaches under Cadence's dress, tugging down her knickers. "So fucking yummy."

"Too much talking." Cadence pushes Marlee onto her knees. "Use your tongue for something else instead."

Dropping Cadence's knickers to her ankles, Marlee gathers the hem of the dress up around her hips, exposing her bare cunt. She's glistening, her labia engorged with blood, plump and ready for Marlee's mouth. In preparation, Cadence steps out of her knickers and hooks a leg over Marlee's shoulder, opening herself up.

"We have to be so much more careful than this," Marlee warns her, teasing her clit with the very tip of her tongue. "We mustn't take any unnecessary risks." She pulls apart Cadence's folds and kisses the slit. "Not when we're so close to making this legal."

"But I like it." Cadence holds Marlee's face to the mark.

Honestly, so does Marlee. In just one day—with the announcement of Cadence's engagement—her employment contract will be over. This is likely to be their last illicit encounter, and it doesn't look like it's going to last long.

As Marlee works her to peak, Cadence's legs become weak, and she finds it difficult to keep herself upright, relying on the wall and Marlee's shoulder for support.

"I'm coming," she whispers frantically, using her free hand to prop herself up on Marlee's other shoulder. "Oh, Marlee ... oh ..." She starts to whimper quietly, her breathing reduced to shallow panting until she's holding her breath completely, tremors engulfing her.

She doesn't let the trapped air out of her lungs until her orgasm passes, releasing her back to reality as she slides down onto Marlee's lap.

"All better?" Marlee smirks, licking all trace of Cadence off her lips.

"For now." Cadence hugs Marlee's neck, and they share a sex-flavored kiss that's abruptly broken by a knock on the cubicle door.

Rat-a-tat-tat. "Is everything all right in there?"

Cadence attempts to stifle a giggle, but ends up snorting, leaving Marlee to try and answer the sales girl without sounding suspicious.

"We're fine, thank you. Stuck zip. Problem solved."

That appears to satisfy her and she leaves, Cadence's giggles exploding as soon as she's presumed to be out of earshot.

"You're dreadfully ill-behaved," Marlee reprimands her lightheartedly. "But you're so desirable." She suppresses her laughter by kissing her again. "Stop being so damn desirable."

Following that close call, they make a quick exit from the store. Cadence dashes out first, without making eye contact with anyone, leaving Marlee behind to pay for the dress—which she does with reddened cheeks, wondering if any of the sales staff heard Cadence's climax.

Chapter Twenty-three

DINNER WITH THE ASHLOCKS IS MADE MARKEDLY MORE uncomfortable by the presence of the Cartwright family. Vince tries to make conversation with Cadence, but Cadence shuts him down. Missus Cartwright tries to find some common ground with Missus Ashlock, but fails. Mister Ashlock is only moderately more animated than usual, Marlee's exquisite bust still being the only thing of interest to him at the table. He converses with Mister Cartwright in spurts, discussing mostly matters of finance. It sounds like white noise to everyone else.

Marlee speaks only when she's spoken to, her slip-on shoes discarded beneath the table, her stockinged feet caressing Cadence's bare ones. Every now and again, she trails her foot up Cadence's calf, rubbing the teen's shin on the way back down.

She doesn't notice when Vince drops his napkin on the floor and bends to retrieve it, but she notices the expression on his face when he resurfaces—he's staring straight at her. Is he daring her to say something? To justify it? She says nothing, returning the stare unwaveringly. If he thinks he's going to rattle her, he's got another thing coming. So their feet are touching. So what? What does that prove? Naught. Even if he did hear them screwing this morning, how would he ever back a claim like that up? Marlee's not particularly worried. Still, they seem to be stuck in a stalemate until Missus Ashlock breaks it.

"Marlee," the lousy, bitter woman demands her attention. "I ought to thank you now before I forget."

"Thank me, milady?"

"For agreeing to stay on with us until Cadence's new maid begins." Missus Ashlock pauses to eat a bite of dinner. "I'm sure you were quite looking forward to being a free woman again, but you can rest assured that you'll be well compensated for your trouble."

"It's no trouble, milady." Marlee shares a smile with Cadence. "It's a pleasure."

Wary of drawing Vince's attention, she looks away, Missus Ashlock remaining entirely oblivious to the complicated triangle that's forming right in front of her.

"Even though you'll no longer be functioning strictly as her nanny, you'll be required to chaperone Cadence at all times during the party tomorrow night," she carries on. "I don't want you to let her out of your sight. After all, you know how teenagers can be, and we don't want anyone misbehaving." She glares at her daughter, no doubt referring to the never-to-be-forgotten champagne incident.

If Missus Ashlock says anything after that, Marlee doesn't hear it. She's too busy enjoying the invading memories of several memorable encounters between herself and Cadence that probably epitomize a few other acts of misbehavior that the Ashlocks would quite like to prevent.

Acts such as a frantic groping in a downstairs hallway while Cadence's parents were having dessert one night. Cadence got them both out of the dining room under the pretense of seeking out some ice cream, then promptly thrust a hand up Marlee's skirt. Marlee protested, of course, but all protests died on her lips the second Cadence's keen fingers made contact with her swollen clit.

Feeling moisture seep into her underwear, Marlee pushes the memory aside.

Thankfully, the rest of dinner passes rather uneventfully, and they retire to the drawing room for the remainder of the evening—Marlee included. She and Cadence hold hands all the while, Cadence leading them to a chaise at the edge of the room. They sit together, Cadence's legs over Marlee's lap, Marlee's arm draped around her shoulders.

"Is this too close?" Cadence whispers, wondering if she should retreat slightly.

"No." Marlee whispers back, risking a kiss on the side of her head. "Some level of closeness is always expected."

"You can sit here with me, Cady," Vince offers pitifully, calling to her from a loveseat.

"I'm fine where I am, thanks," Cadence answers without looking at him.

"Frigid bitch," he mutters under his breath.

Cadence hears him, and would bite back a response, only Marlee won't let her.

"Don't." She gives Cadence's shoulders a squeeze. "You and I know different, and that's all that matters. Who cares what he thinks?"

While the adults, including Vince, enjoy a drink—whiskey for the men, brandy for the women—Cadence is offered juice. She looks into the bottom of her glass, smells it, and pulls a face.

"I hate grape juice." She looks at Marlee's brandy. "Can we swap?"

"Ha!" Marlee chuckles. "Even if I had a death wish, you wouldn't like it."

"How do you know? I might love it."

Marlee flits her eyes around the room, making certain no-one's looking. "Fine." She puts her glass to Cadence's glossy, lipstick-coated lips. "Just a small sip."

A small sip is all it takes.

Cadence coughs and sputters, sticking her tongue out and flapping it in the air before gulping down a healthy dose of her grape juice to combat the taste.

"Ugh! That's vile!" She finishes her juice. "It burns."

"I warned you." Marlee rubs and pats her back, helping her recover.

"You *like* that stuff?!"

"It makes me randy." She winks.

"Oh." Cadence sets her empty glass aside and grabs a blanket, covering their laps with it, tucking it up to their shoulders. "Then drink up."

Using the blanket as a shield, Cadence slides her hand over Marlee's chest, stroking the upper swells of her breasts, her fingertips barely sneaking inside the blouse. Marlee should stop her, but she doesn't. In fact, she rather wishes Cadence would move her hand lower and grope her properly. That is, until the blanket slips, revealing Cadence's wandering hand to anyone who might be looking—and Vince *is* looking.

Disgruntled, he decides to retreat to the games room. As he makes his apologies to the adults, he turns to Missus Ashlock.

"By the way"—he pulls something out of his pocket—"I found these in the games room earlier." He dangles a pair of lacy knickers in the air. "I think one of your domestics might be getting up to no good behind your back." He glares at Marlee, tossing the knickers onto a side table. "You really should put a stop to it."

Following his departure, an awkward silence descends but doesn't last. The conjecture begins almost immediately, with the horrified Ashlocks and the intrigued Cartwrights all tossing out suggestions about who the culprit might be.

The longer this conversation goes on, the more heated it gets, and the more uneasy Marlee becomes. Cadence, her hand still pressed over Marlee's chest, can feel her heart rate escalating, and attempts to get them out of the room as quickly and as smoothly as possible.

Making herself yawn, she stretches dramatically and gets off the chaise, declaring that she wants to go to bed.

"Tuck me in!" She grins at Marlee, her hand outstretched.

"You know you're really too old for that," Missus Ashlock reprimands her, afraid of what the Cartwrights might think.

"It's all right." Marlee lets Cadence pull her off the chaise. "I don't mind."

"No," Missus Ashlock puts her foot down. "She's old enough to do things by herself." Her tone is laced with disapproval. "She's practically a woman."

Cadence refuses to get go of Marlee's hand. "Marlee's still my nanny tonight, isn't she? It's not my birthday until tomorrow."

Missus Ashlock can't refute that.

"Good." Cadence leads Marlee away. "Then Marlee's going to take me to bed."

Oh, if only they knew how true that was!

CADENCE LOOKS SO SERENE AND PEACEFUL, ASLEEP IN Marlee's bed, her chestnut hair ruffled and tangled from the tug and pull of rough sex. Just a few minutes ago, before she'd tackled it with a hairbrush, Marlee's hair looked similar: strands tousled and knotted together after being repeatedly fisted and grappled throughout the night.

As of this morning, she's officially released from her employment contract, and Cadence is seventeen. She's no more Cadence's nanny, but her 'companion', as Mister Ashlock wrote in the memo line of the generous 'Thank You' payment he made to her last night. What does that even mean? Is she being paid to be Cadence's friend?

Laughing it off, she finishes dressing in one of her favorite nanny outfits, possibly for the last time, and prepares to get the day started. When she reaches the bedroom door, however, she thinks better of her haste. She doesn't want Cadence to wake alone on her birthday.

Settling on the edge of the bed, she stirs her young lover with shoulder kisses and nibbles. "Wakey-wakey, sleepyhead. It's your special day."

Cadence rolls onto her back, rubbing her eyes. "Is it really finally here?"

"Happy birthday, darling." Marlee tenders her a lip kiss—the first one permitted to them by law.

"We're legal." Cadence grins, this birthday meaning so much more to her than any of the others before it. "Why are you dressed?" She yawns, frowning at Marlee's appearance. "Where are you going?"

"To make you breakfast in bed."

Cadence rolls her eyes. "I don't expect you to keep doing this shit for me, Marlee. You don't have to. Not anymore."

"Let's get one thing clear, shall we?" Marlee moves Cadence's bangs out of her eyelashes. "I'm not doing it because I *have* to, I'm doing it because I *want* to. Anyway, you're going to be in high demand today, and this might be the only chance I get to dote on you before you're monopolized by your family." She reaches under the bed and pulls out a gift box. "Here, you can amuse yourself with this while I'm gone."

She sets the decorated, red-ribboned box on the pillow beside Cadence, kisses her cheek, and hurries off to fix something quick and delicious. At this time of day, squarely between meals, the kitchen is often deserted. The cook will be taking a nap in her room, while the kitchen maid preps vegetables for lunch in the scullery, leaving Marlee with full run of the kitchen. Gathering up a bowl, a knife, a cutting board, and a selection of fruits—strawberries, blackberries, and a mango—she settles on making a fruit salad.

Happy to be alone with her thoughts, and excited to rejoin Cadence in bed as soon as possible, she's in a deep daydream when Rachel sneaks up on her from behind.

"Oi, oi. What's going on 'ere, then?" Rachel plants her hands on her hips, pretending to be annoyed. "Stealing food are we?"

Marlee pays minimal attention to her, focusing instead on the strawberries.

"Cadence isn't up yet." She scoops the cut berries into the bowl. "It's her birthday, so I thought I'd let her sleep in and bring her something nice for breakfast."

The tension between them seems worse every time they run into one another, what with Marlee unable to explain the reason for suddenly terminating their friends with benefits arrangement, and then rather abruptly refraining from spending her free time in the servants' quarters.

"Are we okay, Marl?" Rachel sidles closer. "I feel like we hardly ever see each other anymore, and when we do, it's ... weird." She tries to walk into Marlee's sightline, but Marlee maneuvers to avoid her.

"Why can't you look at me?" She plants both hands on her hips, frustration oozing into her voice. "Did I do something? I feel like you don't even want to be in the same room with me."

"It's not what you think." Marlee struggles to peel a mango.

"Really?" Rachel leans on the counter beside her. "Let's see: I think you're banging someone else, and you're avoiding me. How true does that ring?"

"Not at all," Marlee claims. "I've just been busy, that's all."

"You're such a terrible liar." Rachel grins, elbowing her in the ribs. "You're having it off with someone, so tell me who it is!"

"Yes, do tell."

Vince's voice kills the playful smile on Rachel's lips, and strikes panic into Marlee. While Rachel straightens up and adopts a stance that befits her status, greeting him politely, Marlee keeps her back to him, continuing to prep the mango.

Ignoring Rachel, he stands in the kitchen doorway, his eyes stuck on Marlee. "Who are you making breakfast for, I wonder?"

"Cadence, sir." Marlee answers without looking up.

"And where is Cadence?" He steps into the kitchen, determined to rattle her. "I was looking forward to wishing her a happy birthday, but she didn't attend breakfast."

"She's sleeping in." Still no eye contact.

"Really? I went to her room, but she wasn't there." He approaches her with a confident swagger. "Have you any idea whose room she might be in?"

"Mine," Marlee says quite casually. "We're going to have breakfast together."

"Shouldn't that be my prerogative?"

"This is the last birthday I'll get to spend with her." Marlee keeps her back to him, slicing into the mango. "I thought we might be able to enjoy breakfast alone."

She can feel him moving near her, his body heat radiating against her.

"By all means." He thieves a chunk of mango. "Say your goodbyes as you please." He bites into the fruit, grinning. "I've no wish to deprive you of such a fleeting pleasure. After all, she'll be out of your hands soon enough."

Marlee doesn't take another breath until he leaves, his presence oppressive.

"What's his problem?" Rachel snorts. "Why's he acting all jealous like you're ..." Her voice trails off, a suspicion sprouting. "No!" She turns to Marlee, her eyes wide. "You're never?!"

Marlee doesn't deny it.

"I thought we were being so careful." She leans on the counter, cursing herself for having been so overconfident. "Turns out it's a lot harder to conceal a love affair when there's actually someone around who's paying attention."

Rachel's jaw flaps for a while before any words come out, and when they do, her voice is so shrill it's almost a screech: high pitched and loud.

"You're diddling Cadence Ashlock?!"

"Quiet!" Marlee gestures to lower her voice. "I'm not diddling her," she whispers. "I'm just ... oh, fuck it." She needs to unburden herself. "If you must know, I've somehow fallen very much in love with her."

170

Silence.

Rachel rolls that around in her head for a while before reaching a verdict on the matter. "I think a tipple is in order."

Marlee checks the clock. "It's ten o'clock in the morning."

"So it is, and you look like a woman who could use some booze."

Rachel drags a chair over to a crockery cabinet and stands on top of it, fumbling for something hidden above: a bottle of the cook's most expensive dry sherry.

"Ta-da!" She wields it proudly, promptly hopping back down to the floor. "Go on, grab us some glasses."

Marlee grabs two from the draining board and sits at the table, Rachel taking a seat opposite her. What kind of lecture is she about to receive? Does Rachel think she's a pervert? Why shouldn't she? This is hardly conventional. Ugh, this is embarrassing.

"So you're diddling Miss Cadence, huh?" Rachel sighs. "That explains a few things." She pours Marlee a generous measure of sherry. "Like why that bloody girl keeps giving me the evils every time she sees me."

Marlee nods. "I'm sorry. I've been terribly unfair to you. Cady was jealous when she saw us together that time, and I tried to make things easy for her by not seeing you anymore." She accepts the glass. "I suppose I've been avoiding you, but I didn't know what else to do. I had to make some compensation for her age."

"Hmm." Rachel pours herself a measure. "And what's that like? Tending to the emotional needs of a sixteen-year-old?"

"She'd never been in that position before: being jealous of someone romantically. She was too young to cope with all the adult feelings she was suddenly having, and the easiest solution was for me to pull away from my friendship with you."

Rachel raises an eyebrow. "But she wasn't too young to get two fingers deep in her nanny?"

"Believe me"—Marlee stares into the bottom of her drink—"I know how bad this looks. I stuck my fingers in a girl under my care. It's not exactly my proudest moment." She downs her sherry, then reaches for the bottle.

"Steady on, Marl."

"If I had any modicum of control over this, I'd have waited until she was eighteen before I let anything happen between us." She refills her glass. "But given the circumstances of her life, that was hardly an option. I always knew she'd be snatched away from me by some awful boy, and ... good god." She takes a sip. "Give me enough time and I'm sure I can find a hundred different ways to justify it. None of which excuse me from the fact that I could've gone to prison for what I've done." Another sip.

Rachel snorts. "Bugger that now. The girl's of age, and you ain't her nanny. What about her parents, though? Are you gonna tell 'em?" Rachel's full of questions. "How are you gonna stop 'em from marrying her off to that snotty little Cartwright kid? It's not like they can just call off the engagement willy-nilly. Not even if they wanted to, which I'm pretty sure they don't."

"Why not?"

"They've signed contracts, yeah? The penalties for breaching will be too harsh, and they'd never let their only child off the hook for a lowly domestic." Rachel looks down into her drink, knowing that's not what Marlee wants to hear. "No offense."

Marlee swirls her sherry, tempted to knock another glass back in one gulp. It hadn't occurred to her that there'd be a breach clause in Cadence's marriage contract—how stupidly naïve of her!—but since the Ashlocks aren't going to have any say in the matter anyway, the fine print is neither here nor there.

She lifts her glass to her lips, taking a shaky gulp. "They won't have a choice."

"How's that?"

"Cadence and I are leaving for Scotland in the morning: the annual long weekend. We'd normally be accompanied by the Ashlocks, of course, but since it's supposed to be our last few days together before Cadence's new maid gets here, they thought we might like to have a few days to ourselves."

"Any excuse." Rachel huffs derisively.

"The thing is, we were rather counting on their lazy parenting this time," Marlee confesses. "Because we've arranged to be married."

She finishes her second sherry and makes a grab for the bottle, but Rachel moves it out of her grasp, eyes wide and jaw dropped.

"Are you having me on?!"

Marlee shakes her head. "The registry office is booked, and I've been hiding wedding rings in my sock drawer for months."

"You sneaky old mare!" Rachel chugs her sherry, slamming the empty glass down on the table with celebratory gusto. "Are you coming back from up north? Or are you taking off with her? All romantic like."

"I just bought a house in Hampshire." Marlee lets a small smile escape. "I'm mortgaged up to my earholes, and we'll be moving in as soon as I get the keys." She hides her trembling hands by folding them in her lap. "I think this is what's known as an elopement." Her smile fades. "You don't think I'm an awful human being for doing this?"

"For doing what?" Rachel pulls a face. "For loving a girl who ain't never got enough from anyone else? For saving her from that frightful pig of a boy?" She offers Marlee encouragement by patting her arm. "You really wanna know what I think? Sod the bleeding Ashlocks. It's about time someone stuck it up 'em!"

Chapter Twenty-five

MARLEE RETURNS TO THE BEDROOM AN INVIGORATED woman after her talk with Rachel. She and Cadence enjoy a light breakfast of sliced and diced fruit, some buttered toast, and two tall glasses of orange juice, then relish their first taste of completely legal sex.

As it happens, the excitement of engaging in repercussion-free love has a decidedly aphrodisiac effect on both of them, and the first round, while vigorous, lasts only minutes. The second round lasts considerably longer, and results in a rather large damp patch on the bed between Marlee's legs, forcing them to huddle together on the other side of the mattress.

"How dare that little turd call me frigid," Cadence grumbles, sprawled naked over Marlee, reflecting on Vince's snide insult from last night.

"You *should* be frigid," Marlee reminds her. "You're far more experienced than you ought to be at your age, and that's entirely my fault."

Remembering a time when Cadence's parents vehemently instructed her not to give their daughter any form of sexual education whatsoever, she snickers. Not only has she drastically failed to comply with that request, but the education she's given Cadence over the last twelve months has been exemplary.

Unfortunately, opportunities to further that education prove to be somewhat few and far between

175

for the rest of the day. As Marlee feared, Cadence's time is first dominated by her parents, then she's forced to drink tea with Mister and Missus Cartwright before spending a quiet afternoon with Vince. By the time she and Marlee get to be alone again, it's much too late for another tumble. She has to get ready for her party, and it's Marlee's job to make sure she looks presentable.

In the bathroom adjoining Marlee's bedroom, Cadence—her hair tamed into a braid—stands in front of the mirror, admiring her reflection. The gift box Marlee handed to her that morning is abandoned in the tub, its contents pillaged, the red ribbon dangling from the bath taps, and she's sporting a brand new set of lacy undies: red with velvet hearts.

The sheer fabric conceals very little. It shows off the pink circles of her areolae, her nipples obscured by two perfectly positioned hearts, and there's a peek of dark pubic hair framing a larger heart at her crotch. As Marlee watches her from the bathroom doorway, two small bumps project from the hearts on Cadence's chest, her nipples stiffening beneath.

"They look good on you." Marlee smiles.

"I love them." Cadence adjusts her bra straps. "When did you sneak out to get them?"

"I have my ways." Marlee swoops in behind her, reaching around her waist.

"Was I sleeping?"

"Maybe." Marlee kisses her shoulder. "Maybe you were exhausted from our energetic lovemaking." She nuzzles her neck, laying kisses there. "Or maybe I paid one of the junior staff to run a little errand for me." She winks at Cadence's reflection.

"Thank you."

"Don't thank me, sweetheart." Marlee trails her hands up, cupping Cadence's breasts. "It's an utterly selfish gift." She targets the two protruding bumps. "I just wanted to see you wearing them."

"That's funny." Cadence smirks. "I just want to see you taking them off."

"And I will, but *after* the party." Marlee drags her out of the bathroom. "Now get your dress on. We're already running behind."

"Tonight almost feels like a proper engagement party." Cadence is positively glowing as she slips into her new dress. "I'm all aflutter."

Marlee zips her up. "Remember to pack this dress tonight." She pats it down and fixes the sash. "I'd like you to wear it when I make you my wife."

Cadence spins to face her, giddy with excitement. "I can't wait!"

"It won't be long." Marlee kisses her, savoring their last few moments of privacy before heading down to the party. "Now, let's get this over with." She ushers the birthday girl toward the door.

They descend the main staircase together, footsteps in synch, and stand outside the main doors to the ballroom, holding hands, hesitant to enter, as if waiting for divine intervention. The party guests are already gathered inside: Cadence's school friends mostly, along with the Ashlocks and the Cartwrights.

"Everyone's going to stare at me." Cadence fidgets in her dress, adjusting the sash, picking her knickers out of her butt crack.

"Of course they are." Marlee steps in front of her, making a few last minute tweaks to her hair. "You'll be the most beautiful woman in the room."

"I don't know about that." Cadence ogles her. "You look really sexy, Marlee."

Marlee looks down at herself: just another nanny ensemble.

"I always wear this." She picks at her skirt.

"I know." Cadence smirks, leaning in for a kiss.

Marlee accepts the intimacy at first, but puts a swift end to it. "Not here."

"But it's my birthday." Cadence puts on an exaggerated pout. "Aren't you supposed to give me anything and everything I want?"

"Gladly. As long as it's not something that's likely to get us both into trouble right before we ... well, you know." Marlee's eyes twinkle. "Patience, darling."

Knowing better than to push her luck and cause a fuss, Cadence drops the topic of kisses and reaches to fumble with Marlee's pinned up hair.

"Ow!" Marlee flinches as Cadence tugs on her locks. "What're you doing?"

"I want you to let your hair down." Cadence drops her hands to Marlee's shoulders. "I hate the way my father looks at you when your hair's up. He's always staring at your tits."

"What can I say? I have nice tits." Marlee smiles cheekily, removing hairpins, shaking out her mane. "Now come on, we have to get you in there before they send a search party out for you. I'd be a terrible chaperone if I couldn't even get you to the party in the first place." She shoves Cadence toward the doors, making her squeal as she feels her rump.

"Tsk, tsk, Marlee." Cadence wags a finger at her, grinning. "That's naughty touching."

Cadence enters the room backwards, pushing the doors open with her bum. Almost immediately, a cacophony of ear piercing squeals and squawks rises above the sound of Cadence's favorite music, and she's bombarded by a gaggle of teenage girls. They gather around her so tightly that Vince can't get within ten feet of her—win!

The girls want to pull her away into their clique, grabbing and tugging on her, but she seems reluctant to go. She doesn't say anything, but she looks over her shoulder, and Marlee can see the conflict in her eyes: torn between staying beside her lover and going with her friends.

"Go," Marlee encourages her. "Go be a carefree teenager."

"Are you sure?" Cadence's brow creases. "I don't want to ditch you."

"This is *your* party. Go, darling."

Marlee shoos her away, watching her disappear in a sea of ball gowns. Should she feel guilty for taking her away from all of this? A girl should be near her friends. A girl *needs* her friends, doesn't she? However will Cadence cope in a strange, new place with no familiar faces? Problems like these call for liquor, Marlee thinks, making her way over to the bar.

She orders up a double measure of gin and perches on a stool, but barely gets the glass to her lips—no chance to take a sip—before she's blindsided by Missus Ashlock.

"Who's she sleeping with?" Cadence's mother sits beside her. "Tell me."

"Excuse me, milady?" Marlee sets down her glass, trying to stay cool and collected.

"I know she's seeing someone." Missus Ashlock speaks in hushed tones. "I know she's fucking him, whoever he is, and I know he was here last night. So who is he? And how long has this been going on?"

Marlee is stuck for words. "How do you ... ?"

"I know you keep her secrets." Missus Ashlock looks around, making sure the Cartwrights aren't within earshot. "I know she tells you everything, so don't lie to me."

"I wouldn't dare, milady." Marlee takes a long, much-needed sip of her gin.

"So who is he?" Missus Ashlock persists. "Is it one of the staff? I hope it's not that blasted stable boy again."

"She's not sleeping with any boy," Marlee assures her—and it's not a lie. It's not the complete truth, either, but it's definitely not a lie.

"Those were her knickers Vince found in the games room, weren't they? I can't imagine they belong to a domestic. Domestics aren't allowed up there." Missus Ashlock raps her press-on nails against the mahogany bar. "Where did she get them? Did you buy them for her?"

"No, I didn't." Marlee picks her drink off the bar and gets up. "Because they're mine."

Walking out on Missus Ashlock in the middle of a conversation—undoubtedly leaving her with more questions than answers—is really quite thrilling. Marlee keeps a steady pace across the room, trying to act like the exchange was nothing out of the ordinary, even though she'd never before have dared to speak to the Missus so curtly.

Adrenalin pumping, she finds somewhere quiet to sit at the edge of the room, inadvertently placing herself in the middle of a row of chairs reserved for wallflowers: those seeking to dance, but who've not yet been asked. Of course, within seconds of bum hitting upholstery, a gentleman in his mid-fifties approaches her.

Presumably, he's the father—divorced, one would hope—of someone in Cadence's group of friends. He asks her to dance, she declines, and he moves on to other targets, the rejection rolling off him like water off the proverbial duck. Randy bastard, Marlee thinks, smirking to herself as he hits on a middle-aged blonde standing by the buffet table.

The whole back-and-forth lasts less than fifteen seconds, but Cadence has her eye on them from beginning to end and breaks away from her cluster of rowdy besties as soon as she can. Dashing across the dance floor, weaving through flailing, twirling bodies, she rather boldly plants herself on Marlee's lap, flinging both arms around her neck.

"Have I ever told you that my friends think you're dead gorgeous?" She plants a kiss on Marlee's cheek. "Because they do, and you damn well are."

"Flatterer." Marlee puts an arm around Cadence's waist, holding her delicately and discreetly, hyper aware that Vince is eyeballing them from a short distance away. "Aren't you worried that your friends will think you have an attachment problem if they see you clinging to your old nanny like this?"

Cadence shrugs. "Who cares what they think? I'd rather be here with you, defending you against the repulsive advances of horny old men."

"My darling savior." Marlee nibbles playfully on her bare shoulder. "Why weren't you here to defend me from your mother a few minutes ago?"

"Ah, is that why you're on the gin?" Cadence teases, flicking the glass with her finger.

"I needed something." Marlee finishes it and sets the glass on an empty chair beside them, resting her hand on Cadence's lap. "I'm all nerves tonight as it is, and she just gave me the third degree."

"About what?"

"Oh, this and that." Marlee rubs her thumb over Cadence's thigh, trying to do so subtly. "She wants to know who you're having sex with."

Cadence rolls her eyes. "She thinks the knickers Vince found are mine?"

"Not anymore." Marlee exploits the angle of Cadence's body to sneak her fingertips beneath the hem of the satin dress, tickling bare thigh. "I told her they were mine."

"Really?!" Cadence titters excitedly. "Who does she think you're doing it with?"

"Cadence," Vince interrupts them before Marlee can answer. "Would you like to dance with me?" He places a hand on her shoulder. "I think it's expected of us."

"Not now." Cadence shrugs him off. "Maybe later."

Their engagement hasn't been announced yet, so she wants to keep him at bay for as long as possible. She doesn't fancy having his cologne-drenched body anywhere near hers, his sweaty palms touching her all over. Ugh. She would quite like to dance, though, and as the music changes to a slow, romantic number, she jumps to her feet, yanking on Marlee's hand.

"Let's dance!"

Warning bells that Marlee had thought long since silenced start to go off again, but she convinces herself that it's all perfectly innocent and above board. What could be the harm? It's just a dance, and there's no reason at all why the two of them shouldn't be seen dancing together.

Indeed, it certainly begins innocently enough, with Cadence's hands on Marlee's shoulders, Marlee's hands on Cadence's waist, and a respectful distance between them. That distance starts to narrow, though, until they're practically pressed against one another, with Cadence's arms wrapped around Marlee's neck, and Marlee's hands on Cadence's lower back.

"Are you happy, darling?" Marlee's now close enough to give her an Eskimo kiss.

"I will be once we're away from here."

They never completely pull back from the nose rub, and their dancing slows ... and slows ... and slows, until they're barely moving. The rest of the room fades away, the music of little importance, and Cadence tilts her head slightly, her lips parted and moist, ready for kissing.

"I love you, Marlee," she whispers, their lips brushing together.

Time grinds to a halt.

People must be staring.

Marlee knows the kiss is coming long before it happens, and she does nothing to stop it. In fact, she welcomes it. She *wants* the Ashlocks to see her with their daughter, and for them to know that, for all their wealth and influence, they have no control over Cadence's heart—nor who she chooses to give it to.

Eyes closed, she feels the heat from Cadence's breath as their mouths press together, the intimate peck lasting for a full five seconds.

One.

Two.

Three.

Four.

Five.

That should be it. That should be the end of it, but Marlee keeps her eyes closed, waiting for more, blaming the gin for throwing caution to the wind.

"That's not enough," she whispers breathily, letting her hands slip from Cadence's waist to her bum, squeezing her buttocks. "I want more."

As the words tumble off the tip of her tongue, she becomes aware of Cadence's arms tightening around her neck and the warmth returning to her lips. Another kiss!

It begins tentatively, lips pinched against lips, then it evolves into more, the intensity escalating until they're in the midst of a passionate clinch. They're not dancing at all, they're just kissing—in front of *everyone.*

Five seconds.

Ten.

Fifteen.

Twenty.

Wow.

In the wake of it, Marlee—surprisingly calm, given the circumstances—smiles broadly. "I think we might have to leave now." She takes Cadence's hands in hers. "I hope you're packed!"

The next few minutes pass as if they're caught up in a tumbling wave: riding the crest of it, caught up in the swell of it, going with the flow of it. While the Ashlocks and Cartwrights turn their tempers on one another, flinging accusations like monkeys hurl shit, Marlee and Cadence flee from the room.

After retrieving their suitcases, they use the servants' passages to make a stealthy exit through the servants' quarters, where Rachel—all too happy to "Stick it up the Ashlocks!"—helps them escape through the back door, handing them the keys to one of the vehicles licensed for use by the domestic staff.

It all seems so easy.

Drive to the train station.

Ditch the car there.

Buy two tickets to Glasgow with cash.

Marry Cadence.

Live happily ever after.

What could possibly go wrong?

Two months later ...

CADENCE WAKES UP TO AN ABUNDANCE OF SOFT KISSES south of her waist, Marlee's face buried between her thighs. In short order, she giggles with astonishment, moans, clutches at Marlee's tresses, moans again, and comes. From beginning to end, the performance lasts a little under five glorious minutes.

Satisfied with her accomplishment, Marlee resurfaces and settles next to Cadence on the bed, licking her lips. "Good morning, darling. Are you ready for your big day?"

Cadence takes a deep breath, glancing out of the bedroom window at the dark blue hue of the pre-dawn sky. "I think so."

"Up you get, then." Marlee wriggles out of bed, already dressed in jeans and a blouse—this one with proper buttons that go all the way. "I can walk there with you, if you'd like." She pulls the duvet off naked Cadence. "It's sort of on the way for me."

It's been eight weeks since their elopement, and six weeks since they took up residence in their modest, middle-of-the-row terraced house nestled in the picturesque Hampshire village of Beaulieu, just a twenty minute drive from Milford-on-Sea. The cottage is tiny—only two up, two down—but it's all they need. Perhaps more importantly, it's all they can afford.

Marlee was worried that Cadence would find it claustrophobic having to live in such tight quarters, but as yet, she hasn't expressed even the slightest hint of displeasure or discomfort. Much to Marlee's relief, no regrets have surfaced either.

Cadence is adjusting well to her new life, becoming accustomed to doing dishes, helping Marlee make dinner, and tending to their small garden. There've been a few teething problems, of course. For instance, the first time she cleaned the toilet, she threw up all over the floor. The toilet wasn't even dirty. It was just a practice run.

Fortunately, Marlee's parents are close enough for regular visits. Her mother's been good about teaching Cadence how to cook and change lightbulbs, while her father's been offering up tips on vegetable growing. They've taken Cadence under their wing, showering her with all the love and attention she never received from her own mother and father as a child.

It's a perfect life, and Marlee hums contentedly, making Cadence a breakfast of jam-slathered toast. She's been trying to mother her less, but it's difficult. The habit of caring for her is just too deeply ingrained. Not that she really minds. She likes doing things for her young lover—now her wife.

Wife! What a thought! She twirls a sterling silver wedding ring around her finger, admiring the simple elegance of it, still getting used to the idea.

"It's not a dream, Marl." Cadence smiles at her from the kitchen doorway. "It really happened." She holds up her left hand, showing off a matching ring.

She looks very grown up, Marlee thinks, gazing at her in black cotton trousers and a white blouse, her hair braided by her own hand, a trace of shadow on her eyelids.

"Well, I hope you won't mind if I continue to be amazed by it every day." Marlee hands her a plate of toast. "Amazed, and extraordinarily happy."

Cadence takes the plate. "I can make my own toast, you know. I learned how to work the toasting contraption while we were in Scotland."

"And you only set the smoke alarm off once." Marlee laughs. "Very impressive."

"I'm glad you appreciate my talents, and just think"—Cadence sits at their small table, handmade by Marlee's father—"this time next year, I might even be able to use the oven."

"We'll see about that. I'm not sure you can be trusted." Still laughing, Marlee glances at the clock on the wall. "Oh, heck! We'd better get a move on, else you'll be late."

They leave the house in under ten minutes, embarking on the short walk from their humble dwelling to the rear entrance of Palace House: a stately home on the banks of the Beaulieu River.

"This isn't on your way to work at all, is it?" Cadence suspects as they reach the back gates. "Did you walk me here just to make sure I wouldn't bottle it at the last minute?"

"No, you daft bugger." Marlee fixes Cadence's bangs, making sure she looks perfectly presentable. "I mean, you're half right. It's not on my way to work—it's the opposite direction in fact—but I only came because I thought you'd like the company."

Cadence scoops her into an embrace and kisses her softly. "I love the company." Another kiss. "Will you meet me here after? We'll walk home together."

"Of course, sweetheart." One more kiss.

That would be their parting, but as Cadence turns to walk through the gates, Marlee notices there's something amiss.

"Wait." She captures Cadence's elbow, holding her back. "You're missing something." She waggles a finger at her blouse, just above her left breast. "Where is it? You haven't forgotten it already, have you?"

"Nope!" Cadence digs around in her trouser pockets, finally fishing out a nametag. "You do the honors." She hands it over.

Marlee fixes the tag to her blouse, making sure it's not wonky. "All better." She taps her bum lightly. "Now get inside."

Cadence does as she's told, looking over her shoulder no less than four times between the gates and the Palace House servants' entrance. She's nervous, but doing her best to hide it.

Today marks the first day of her first ever job, and truthfully, Marlee *had* half feared she might succumb to nerves and back out. This is such a far cry from the life she was meant to lead: working as a maid instead of having one of her own.

Certainly, over the last few years, Cadence has made some brave choices, and Marlee wonders if, in her position—especially at her age—she'd have had the courage to do the same. At seventeen, she was still seeing boys and trying to figure out why they didn't make her heart go thump-thump like they did with her friends. It took her another year to figure that one out.

At any rate, she walks back the way she came— back into the center of the village—and heads toward the independent children's nursery she now works at, caring for a classroom full of preschool age children.

Life couldn't be better.

Meanwhile, at Neverleigh Manor, the penny still hasn't dropped. Once the shock dissipated and the yelling subsided, the Ashlocks burst into laughter. In their eyes, this little "stunt" is just another one of Cadence's tantrums.

When they caught up to the runaways in Glasgow, they didn't fight to take Cadence back. Instead, they arrived with a small truck containing all of Cadence's worldly possessions.

She was free to "explore her delusions," they'd said smugly, feeling confident that the real world would soon kick some sense into her.

Along with her belongings, they handed her marriage annulment paperwork, so that when she's had enough, she can clear up her mess and come crawling back to the family estate with her tail between her legs, ready to satisfy their contractual obligations by accepting Vince as her husband.

They still believe her marriage to Marlee is a sham, and Marlee can't help but wonder how they'll feel when Cadence fails to return home after three, four, five, six months, and continues to thrive outside the bubble of their money.

Moreover, she'd love to see the looks on their faces when the Cartwrights finally lose their patience and slap them with a breach of contract lawsuit to the tune of two point five million pounds—some small punishment for their cruelty and ignorance.

The End

About the Author

Keira Michelle Telford is an award-winning author with a love for the gruesome, the macabre, and the downright filthy. She writes historical and contemporary erotic sapphic romance, and other sapphic fiction.

Erotic Lesbian Romance
The Housemistress

Historical Lesbian Romance
The Ruin of Us
Quicunque Vult
Never Come to Rest

Short Stories
Hoar & Rime
Evonnia & the Maiden
Falling Hard

Futanari
All the Devils (short story)
Come, My Pet

Website: www.keiramichelle.com
Twitter: @km_telford
Facebook: www.facebook.com/keiramichelletelford
Goodreads: www.goodreads.com/keiramichelle
Amazon: www.amazon.com/author/keiramichelle